Dark-Hearted

Many years ago there were t~~~~
ruled as one kingdom—Ada~~~~
ripped the kingdom apart an~~~~
separately. The Greek Karedes family reigned supreme
over glamorous Aristo, and the smoldering Al'Farisi sheikhs
commanded the desert lands of Calista!

When the Aristan king died, an illegitimate daughter
was discovered—Stefania, the rightful heir to the throne.
Ruthlessly the Calistan sheikh Zakari seduced her into
marriage to claim absolute power but was overawed by her
purity and succumbed to love. Now they rule both Aristo
and Calista together, in the spirit of hope and prosperity.

But a black mark hangs over the Calistan royal family
still. As young boys, three of King Zakari's brothers were
kidnapped for ransom by pirates. Two safely returned,
but the youngest was swept out to sea and never found—
presumed dead. Then at Stefania's coronation, a stranger
appeared in their midst. The ruler of a nearby kingdom—
Qusay. A stranger with scars on his wrists from the pirates'
ropes. A stranger who knows nothing of his past—only
his future as a king!

What will happen when Xavian, King of Qusay,
discovers that he's living the wrong life? And who will
claim the Qusay throne if the truth is unveiled?

**Find out in the brand-new
Harlequin Presents® miniseries**

Dark-Hearted Desert Men

*One Kingdom. One Crown. Four smoldering desert
princes…Which one will claim the throne
and who will they claim as their brides?*

Book 1: *Wedlocked: Banished Sheikh, Untouched Queen*
by Carol Marinelli
Book 2: *Tamed: The Barbarian King* by Jennie Lucas
Book 3: *Forbidden: The Sheikh's Virgin* by Trish Morey
Book 4: *Scandal: His Majesty's Love-Child* by Annie West

Annalisa narrowed her eyes against the setting sun

A shadow. More than a shadow. A man. She made out broad shoulders and dark clothes. Remarkably, for this place, he was wearing what looked like a suit as he took a step down the dune, letting the slip of sand carry him several meters.

But as she watched his slow progress she realized something was wrong. Instincts honed by years of helping her father tend to the sick overrode her wariness. The stranger was no threat. He looked as if he could barely stay upright. Moments later she was racing toward him.

Her steps slowed as she neared and took in the full impact of his appearance.

Her breath hissed in her throat. Disbelief filled her. She blinked, but the image was clear and unmistakable.

A tall man, dark haired, wearing a tuxedo and black leather shoes, was slipping down the dune toward her. His dress shirt was ripped open and filthy, revealing bronzed skin and the top of a broad chest. A dark ribbon, the end of a bow tie, fluttered against his collarbone.

His face was long and lean and so caked in sand she could barely make out his features. Yet the solid shape of his jaw and the high angle of his cheeks hinted at a devastating masculine beauty. His temple was a mass of dried blood that made her suck in a dismayed breath.

But it was his eyes that held her still as he slithered down the slope. Piercing blue, they mesmerised her. Such an unexpected color here in a desert kingdom.

Annie West

SCANDAL: HIS MAJESTY'S LOVE-CHILD

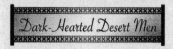

Dark-Hearted Desert Men

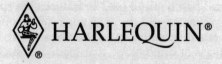

HARLEQUIN®

TORONTO • NEW YORK • LONDON
AMSTERDAM • PARIS • SYDNEY • HAMBURG
STOCKHOLM • ATHENS • TOKYO • MILAN • MADRID
PRAGUE • WARSAW • BUDAPEST • AUCKLAND

With special thanks and acknowledgments given to Annie West for her contribution in the Dark-Hearted Desert Men continuity

Recycling programs
for this product may
not exist in your area.

ISBN-13: 978-0-373-12928-7

SCANDAL: HIS MAJESTY'S LOVE-CHILD

First North American Publication 2010.

All about the author...
Annie West

ANNIE WEST discovered romance early—her childhood best friend's house was an unending store of Harlequin® books—and she's been addicted ever since. Fortunately she found her own real-life romantic hero while studying at university and married him. Despite the distraction she completed an honors degree in classics. Annie took a job in the public service. For years she wrote and redrafted and revised government plans, letters for cabinet ministers and reports for parliament. Checking the text of a novel is so much more fun! Annie started to write romance fiction when she took leave to spend time with her children. Between school activities she produced her first novel. At the same time she discovered Romance Writers of Australia. Since then she's been active in RWAus writers' groups and competitions. She attends annual conferences and loves the support she gets from so many other writers. Her first Harlequin novel came out in 2005.

Annie lives with her hero (still the same one) and her children at Lake Macquarie, north of Sydney, where she spends her time fantasizing about gorgeous men and their love lives. It's hard work, but she has no regrets!

Annie loves to hear from readers. You can contact her via her Web site, www.annie-west.com, or e-mail her at annie@annie-west.com.

Carol, Jennie and Trish.
It was terrific working with you.
Thank you!

CHAPTER ONE

'PLACE your bets, *mesdames et messieurs*.'

Sheikh Tahir Al'Ramiz glanced around the gaming table, at the crowd watching him with rapt attention, eager to see his next move. His gaze trawled past the stack of chips he'd won in the last hour.

A waiter hovered with a fresh bottle of champagne. Tahir nodded and turned to the woman pressed so eagerly against his side. Blonde, beautiful, accommodating. She'd turned heads from the moment they entered Monte Carlo's opulent old casino.

She moved and the fortune in diamonds encircling her throat and dripping down her superb cleavage flashed in the chandelier's mellow light. Her stunning evening dress of beaded silver was testament to the effect wealth and a world-class couturier could achieve.

She smiled, the sort of intimate, eager smile women had been giving him since adolescence.

He passed her a flute of France's finest champagne and leant back in his seat, finally acknowledging what he'd felt all evening.

He was bored.

Last time it had taken him two days to tire of Monte Carlo. This time he'd just arrived.

'Last bets, *mesdames et messieurs*.'

Stifling a sigh, Tahir caught the croupier's eye. *'Quatorze,'* he said.

The croupier nodded and moved Tahir's chips.

A hush fell as the crowd sucked in its collective breath. People on the other side of the table hurried to follow his lead, placing last-minute bets.

'Fourteen?' said the blonde, eyes widening. 'You're betting it *all* on one number?'

Tahir shrugged and lifted his glass. Idly he noted how the faint tremor in his hand made the surface of the wine ripple.

How long since he'd slept? Two days? Three? There'd been New York, where he'd finally closed that media deal and stayed to party. Then Tunisia for some all-terrain racing, Oslo and Moscow for more business, then here to his cruiser in the marina.

Was his lifestyle finally catching up with him?

He tried to dredge up some interest, some concern, and failed.

With a flourish the croupier set the roulette wheel spinning.

Slender fingers gripped Tahir's knee through the fine wool of his trousers. His companion's breathing quickened as the wheel spun. Her hand slipped up his thigh.

Did she find the thrill of gambling, even by proxy, so arousing?

He almost envied her. Tahir knew that if she were to strip naked and offer herself to him here and now, he'd feel nothing. No desire. No excitement. *Nothing*.

She flashed him another smile, a sultry invitation, and leaned close, her breast pressing against his arm.

He really should remember her name.

Elsa? Erica? It eluded him. Because he hadn't been interested enough to fix it in his mind? Or because his memory was becoming impaired?

His lips quirked briefly. Unfortunately his memory still functioned perfectly.

Some things he'd never forget.

No matter how hard he tried.

Elisabeth. That was it. Elisabeth Karolin Roswitha, Countess von Markburg.

Clamorous applause roused him from his thoughts. A cushioned embrace engulfed him as the Countess von Markburg almost climbed onto his lap in her excitement. Soft lips grazed his cheek, his mouth.

'You've won again, Tahir!' She pulled back, her eyes glittering with excitement. 'Isn't it marvellous?'

He moved his lips in what passed for a smile and raised his glass.

Tahir envied her that simple rush of pleasure. How long since he'd experienced that? Gambling didn't do it for him any more. Business coups? Sometimes. Extreme sports? At least he got an adrenalin rush when he put his neck on the line. Sex?

He watched another woman approach. A dark-haired seductress wearing ruby drop earrings that brushed her bare shoulders and a dress that would have her locked up for indecency in a lot of countries.

And he felt not a flicker of response.

She stopped beside him, leaned down, giving him a view right down her dress, past unfettered breasts to her navel and beyond.

'Tahir, darling. It's been an age.'

Her lips opened against his and her tongue slicked along the seam of his lips. But he wasn't in the mood.

Fatigue suddenly swamped him. Not physical tiredness, but the insidious grey nothingness that had plagued him so long.

He was tired of life.

Abruptly he pulled back from her hungry kiss. It was only months since they'd been together in Buenos Aires yet it felt a lifetime ago.

'Elisabeth.' He turned to the blonde still glued to his side. 'Let me introduce Natasha Leung. Natasha, this is Elisabeth von Markburg.'

He nodded to the waiter, who produced another champagne flute.

'Ah, it's my favourite vintage,' Natasha purred, standing closer, so her thigh slid against his. 'Thank you.'

Over her shoulder Tahir caught the croupier's expressionless gaze.

'Place your bets, *s'il vous plait.*'

'*Quatorze,*' Tahir murmured.

'*Quatorze?*' The croupier's impeccable reserve couldn't hide the astonishment in his eyes. '*Oui, monsieur.*'

'Fourteen again?' Elisabeth's voice rose shrilly. 'But you'll lose it all! The chances of getting the same number again are impossible.'

Tahir shrugged and, alerted by a discreet ring tone, dragged his mobile phone from his pocket. 'Then I'll lose.'

At the look of horror on her face Tahir almost smiled. Life was so simple for some.

He looked at the phone, frowning when he didn't recognise the number displayed. Only his lawyer and his most trusted brokers had his private number. This wasn't one of them.

'Hello?'

'Tahir?' Even after so long that voice was unmistakable. Tahir surged to his feet, dislodging both the women clinging to him.

'Kareef.'

Only something truly significant would make his eldest brother call him out of the blue and after so long. He turned his back on the table, gesturing to his companions to stay where they were. The crowd around him parted, as it always did, and he strode across the room to the privacy of a quiet corner.

'This is an unexpected surprise,' he murmured. 'To what do I owe the pleasure?'

Silence. It stretched so long the back of his neck prickled.

'I want you to come home.' Kareef's voice was as calm and familiar as it had always been.

But the words. They were words Tahir had never thought to hear.

'I don't have a home any more. Remember?'

A tiny part of long-dormant conscience told him he took out his old bitterness unfairly on Kareef. His brother wasn't to blame for the disaster that was Tahir's past.

He clamped his mouth shut.

'You do now, Tahir.' Something in his brother's voice sent a tingle of premonition down his spine.

'Our revered father would have something to say to that.'

'Our father is dead.'

The words rolled like thunder in Tahir's brain.

The brute who'd ruled his people and his family so corruptly was gone for ever.

The tyrant who'd betrayed his wife with a string of whores and mistresses. Who'd ruled his tribe by fear. Who'd thrashed Tahir time and again to within an inch of his life. Then had his thugs take over when Tahir grew old enough to defend himself against his father.

The man who'd exiled his youngest son when he'd finally done what the old Sheikh had probably secretly wanted and overstepped the mark completely.

Tahir had never been able to please his father, no matter how he tried. He'd spent his boyhood wondering what fault of his inspired such hatred.

But he'd long ago given up caring.

Tahir turned to look across the elegant room and its throng of late-night pleasure-seekers. In his mind's eye it wasn't the glamorous crowd he saw, the flirtatious and curious glances or the opulent display of wealth. It was Yazan Al'Ramiz's blood-shot eyes, his bristling moustache flecked with spittle as he ranted and bellowed. The violent pounding of his clenched fists.

Surely Tahir should feel something, anything, at the news his tyrant father was dead? Even after eleven years' absence the news must evoke some response?

A yawning void of darkness welled inside where once emotions had lodged.

He supposed he should have questions.

When? How? Wasn't that what a child asked about a father's death?

'Still, I don't feel a burning desire to return to Qusay.' His tone was as blank as his mood. There was nothing for him in the land of his birth.

'Damn it, Tahir. Stop playing the arrogant unfeeling bastard for a moment. I need you here. Things are complicated.' Kareef paused. 'I *want* you here.'

Something unfamiliar roiled deep in Tahir's belly.

'What do you need?' Kareef had always been his favourite brother. The one he'd looked up to, in the long-ago days when he'd still tried to emulate his elders and betters. 'What's the problem?'

'No problem,' Kareef said in a curiously strained voice. 'But our cousin has discovered he isn't the rightful king of Qusay. He's stood aside and I'm to take his place on the throne.' He paused. 'I want you here for my coronation.'

Tahir walked slowly to the roulette table.

Kareef's news was momentous. To discover their cousin had been made King in error was almost unbelievable. He was no blood relation to the old King and Queen, but had been secretly taken in by them while they grieved the death of their real son. If it had been anyone other than Kareef telling the story Tahir would have doubted the news.

But Kareef would never make such an error. He was too careful, too responsible. He would make the perfect King for Qusay. Either of Tahir's older brothers would.

Thank merciful fate their father wasn't alive to inherit the throne! As brother to the old King and leader of a significant clan he'd been too powerful as it was—too dangerous. Having him rule the whole nation would have been like letting a wolf in amongst lambs.

A heart attack, Kareef had said.

No wonder. Their father had liked to indulge himself and hadn't limited himself to one vice.

Tahir approached the gaming table. He saw his barely touched champagne and the two women waiting for him, both undoubtedly eager to give him whatever he desired tonight.

His lips curled. Perhaps he was more like the old man than he realised.

'Tahir!' Elisabeth's voice was a shriek of delight. 'You'll never believe it. You won! Again! It's unbelievable.'

The babbling crowd hushed. Every eye was on him, as if he'd done something miraculous.

Before him, piled high, were his winnings. Far larger than before. The croupier looked pale and rigidly composed.

Eager feminine hands reached for Tahir as his companions sidled close. Their eyes were bright with avarice and excitement.

Tahir slid some of the most valuable chips to the croupier. 'For you.'

'*Merci, monsieur*.' He grinned as he scooped his newfound wealth safely into his hand.

Tahir lifted his glass, took a long swallow and let the bubbles cascade from the back of his tongue down his throat.

The wine's effervescence seeped into him. He felt buoyant, almost happy. For once fate had played things right. Kareef would be the best King Qusay had known.

He put the glass down with a click and turned away.

'Goodnight, Elisabeth, Natasha. I'm afraid I have business elsewhere.'

He'd taken but a few steps when the babble of voices stopped him.

'Wait! Your winnings! You've forgotten them.'

Tahir turned to face a sea of staring faces.

'Keep them. Share them amongst yourselves.'

Without a backward glance he strode to the entrance, oblivious to the uproar behind him.

The doorman thrust open the massive doors and Tahir emerged into the fresh night air. He breathed deep, filling his lungs for the first time, it seemed, in recent memory.

A hint of a smile played on his lips as he loped down the stairs.

He had a coronation to attend.

Tahir skimmed low over the dunes of Qusay's great interior desert.

Alone at the helicopter's controls, he put the effervescence in his blood down to the freedom of complete solitude. No hangers-on. No business minions seeking direction. No women with wide eyes and grasping hands. Not even paparazzi waiting to report his next outrageous affair.

Perhaps the barren glory of the desert had lifted his spirits? He even, for this moment, put from his mind what awaited him in Qusay.

His family. His past.

Yet he'd visited deserts in the last eleven years. From North Africa to Australia and South America, motor-racing, hang-gliding, base-jumping—always searching for new extreme ways to risk his neck.

Finally he recognised his mood was because he flew over the place he'd called home for the first eighteen years of his life. The place he'd never expected to see again.

But this realisation came as an almighty gust buffeted the chopper, slewing it sideways. Tahir grappled with the controls, swinging the helicopter high above the dunes.

The sight that met him sent adrenalin pumping through his body. The growing darkness filling the sky wasn't an early dusk, as he'd thought.

If he'd been flying by the book he'd have noticed the warning signs sooner. Instead he'd been skylarking, swooping dangerously low, gambling on his ability to read the topography of a place that changed with every wind.

This was the mother of all sandstorms. The sort that claimed livestock, altered watercourses and buried roads. The sort that could whip up a helicopter like a toy, whirl it round and smash it into fragments.

No chance to outrun it. No time to land safely.

Nevertheless, Tahir battled to steer the bucking chopper away from the massive storm. Automatically he switched into crisis mode, sending out a mayday, knowing already it was too late.

Calmness stole over him. *He was going to die.*

The prodigal had returned to his just deserts.

He wasn't dead.

Fate obviously had something far worse in store. Dehydration in the heat. Or, going by the pain racking him, death from his wounds.

The preposterous luck that had seen him win several fortunes at the gaming table had finally abandoned him.

Tahir debated whether to open his eyes or lie there, seeking the luxurious darkness of unconsciousness again. Yet the throbbing pain in his head and chest was impossible to ignore.

Even opening his eyes hurt. Light pierced his retinas through sand-encrusted lashes. It dazzled him and he groaned, tasting heat and dust and the metallic saltiness of blood. His hands and face felt raw from exposure to whipping sand.

He had a vague recollection of sitting, blinded by dust and strapped in a seat, hearing the unearthly yowl of wind and lashing sand. Then the smell of petrol, so strong he'd fought free of both seatbelt and twisted metal, stumbling as far as he could.

Then nothing.

Overhead the pure blue of a cerulean sky mocked him.

He was alive. In the desert. Alone.

Tahir passed out three times before he dragged himself to a sitting position, sweating and trembling and feeling more dead than alive. His brain was scrambled, wandering into nothingness and then jerking back to the present with hideous clarity.

He sat with his back against a sandbank, legs stretched out, and tried to ignore the brain-numbing pain that was the back of his skull in contact with sand.

He was drifting into unconsciousness when something jerked him awake. A rough caress on his hand. Gingerly he tilted his head.

'You're a mirage,' he whispered, but the words wouldn't emerge from his constricted throat.

The animal sensed his attention. It stared back, its horizontal pupils dark against golden-brown irises. It shook its head and a cloud of dust rose from its shaggy coat.

'Mmmmah.'

'Mirages don't talk,' Tahir murmured. They didn't lick either. But this one did, its tongue tickling. He shut his eyes, but when he opened them the goat was still there. A kid, too small to be without its mother.

Hell. He couldn't even die in peace.

The goat butted his hip, and Tahir realised his jacket pocket had something in it. Slowly, so as not to black out from the pain, he slipped his hand in and found a water bottle.

A muzzy memory rose, of him grabbing bottled water as he stumbled from the wreckage. How had he forgotten that?

It took for ever to pull the bottle out, twist off the lid and lift it to his lips. The hardest thing he'd ever done was drag it away after one sip.

Guzzling too much was dangerous. He risked another sip then lowered his hand. It felt like a dead weight.

Something nudged him and he opened his eyes to see the goat curled up close. In the whole vast expanse of desert the beast had chosen this place to shelter.

Gritting his teeth as he brought his left hand over his body, Tahir poured water into his palm.

'Here you are, goat.'

Placidly it drank, as if used to human contact. Or as if it too was on its last legs and had no room for fear.

Tahir had just enough energy to recap the bottle before it slid from his shaking hands. His head lolled.

Beside him the warmth of that tiny body penetrated his clothes, reminding him he wasn't alone.

It was that knowledge that forced him to focus on surviving Qusay's notoriously perilous desert.

Annalisa drew water up in the battered metal scoop and sluiced it over her face. Heaven.

The huge sandstorm had delayed her journey into the desert. Her cousins had tut-tutted, saying it was proof this trip was a mistake. The sort of mistake she wouldn't survive. But they didn't understand.

Just six months after her granddad's death, and her beloved father's soon after, it meant everything that she come here.

Annalisa was keeping her last promise to her father.

It was wonderful to be here again, though sadness tinged the experience as she remembered previous trips with her dad.

She'd arrived this morning, spending the afternoon cleaning her camera and telescopic equipment. A day out here meant a day of heat and dust, and the luxury of having the oasis to herself was too much to resist.

She lifted another scoop of water and tipped it over her head, shivering luxuriously as the water slid through her hair, over her shoulders and down her back. Another scoop sluiced over her breasts and she smiled, revelling in the feeling of being clean. She wriggled her toes in the sandy bottom of the small pool.

The sun was setting and she should move to build up the fire before darkness fell.

She was just turning to get out of the water when something on the horizon caught her attention. She narrowed her eyes against the setting sun.

A shadow. More than a shadow. A man. She made out broad shoulders and dark clothes. Remarkably, for this place, he was wearing what looked like a suit as he took a step down the dune, letting the slip of sand carry him several metres.

Automatically Annalisa reached for her towel and wrapped it close, her actions slowing when she registered his strange gait. He didn't use his arms to keep his balance on the treacherously steep slope and his movements were oddly uncoordinated.

Caution warned her to take no chances with a stranger.

No local would harm her. But this man clearly didn't belong. Who knew how he'd react to finding a lone female?

But as she knotted the towel and watched his slow progress she realised something was wrong. Instincts honed by years of helping her father tend to the sick overrode her wariness. The stranger was no threat. He looked as if he could barely stay upright.

Moments later she was racing up the other side of the *wadi* towards him.

Her steps slowed as she neared and took in the full impact of his appearance.

Her breath hissed in her throat. Disbelief filled her. She blinked, but the image was clear and unmistakable.

A tall man, dark-haired, wearing a tuxedo and black leather shoes, was slipping down the dune towards her. His dress shirt was ripped open and filthy, revealing bronzed skin and the top of a broad chest. A dark ribbon, the end of a bow tie, fluttered against his collarbone.

His face was long and lean and so caked in sand she could barely make out his features. Yet the solid shape of his jaw and the high angle of his cheeks hinted at a devastating masculine beauty. His temple was a mass of dried blood that made her suck in a dismayed breath.

But it was his eyes that held her still as he slithered down the slope. Piercing blue, they mesmerised her. Such an unexpected colour here in a desert kingdom.

Even as he staggered towards her his tall frame looked improbably elegant and absurdly raffish. As if he'd drunk too much at a society party and wandered unsteadily off.

Then she registered the way he cradled his arms across his torso and fear escalated. Chest wounds? She could deal with cuts and abrasions. She was her father's daughter after all. But they were days away from medical help and her skills only went so far.

Clumsily Annalisa raced up the dune, hauling the flapping towel tighter. Her heart thudded painfully as she fought to suppress panic.

She'd almost reached him when he stumbled and dropped to his knees, swaying woozily.

He stretched out his arms and looked up from under a tangle of matted dark hair.

'Here, sweetheart.' His voice was a hoarse whisper, thick and slurred, as if his tongue didn't work properly. She leaned closer to hear. 'Take care of it.'

His arms dropped and something, a small scruffy animal, rolled out as the stranger pitched to one side, seemingly lifeless, at her feet.

CHAPTER TWO

ANNALISA sat back on her heels and pushed a lock of hair behind her ear with shaky fingers. She trembled all over, her arms weak as jelly from exertion. Her pulse was still racing from shock and the fear she mightn't be able to save him.

After a quick check she'd decided to risk moving the stranger to her campsite. His temperature was dangerously high and a night on the exposed dune could prove fatal.

But she hadn't reckoned on the logistics of transporting a man well over six feet and at least a head taller than her.

It had taken an hour of strained exertion and all her ingenuity to get him down, dragging him on a makeshift stretcher. Most frightening of all he'd been a dead weight, not stirring.

'Don't you die on me now,' she threatened as she checked his weak pulse and began cleaning the wound on his temple.

Head wounds bled prolifically. It probably wasn't as bad as it looked, she told herself. Yet she found herself muttering a mix of prayer and exhortation in mingled Arabic, Danish and English, just as her dad had used to when faced with a hopeless case.

The familiar words calmed her, made her feel slightly more in control, though she knew that was an illusion. It would be a miracle if her patient pulled through.

'It's okay.' A slurred voice broke across her thoughts. 'I know I won't survive.' His eyes remained closed, but Annalisa watched his bloodied, cracked lips move and knew she hadn't imagined his voice.

Hope surged, and a spark of anger born of fear.

'Don't be ridiculous! Of course you'll live.' He'd echoed her fears so precisely she lashed out, heart pounding in denial.

After a moment his lips moved again, this time in a twitch that might have signified amusement.

'If you say so.' Now his voice was weaker, a thready whisper. 'But don't fret if you're wrong.' He drew a shaky breath that rattled in his lungs. 'I won't mind at all.'

The words trailed off and he lay so still in the lamplight Annalisa couldn't make out his breathing. Frantically she fumbled for his pulse. Relief pounded through her when she felt it.

She told herself it was better he'd slipped into unconsciousness again. He wouldn't feel pain as she tended his wounds.

It was only later, as she placed a damp cloth on his forehead, trying to lower his temperature, that she realised the man had spoken to her in perfect English.

Who was he? And what was a lone foreigner doing in Qusay's arid heartland dressed like some suave movie star?

Tahir ached all over. His head hammered mercilessly, as if a demolition squad had started work inside his skull. His mouth and throat were parched and raw. Swallowing felt like his muscles closed over broken glass. His body was stiff and weighted, bruised all over.

It was one hell of a beating this time, he realised vaguely. *Had the old man finally gone too far?*

Tahir couldn't bring himself to struggle out of the blackness to take in his surroundings. Instinctively he knew the pain would be overwhelming when he did. Right now he didn't have the strength to pretend he didn't care.

His only weapons against his father were pride and feigned unconcern. To meet the old man's eyes steadily and refuse to beg for mercy.

It drove his tormentor wild and robbed him of the satisfaction he sought from lashing out at his son.

No matter how bad the thrashing, how prolonged or vicious, Tahir never begged for it to end. Nor did he cry out. Not a murmur, not a flinch, no matter how remorseless his father's ice-cold eyes or how explosive his temper. Even when Yazan Al'Ramiz brought in thugs to subdue Tahir and prolong the punishment, Tahir refused to give in.

There was triumph in facing down the man who'd hated him for as long as he could remember. That was little recompense for not knowing *why* Yazan loathed him, but it gave him something to focus on rather than go crazy seeking an explanation the old man refused to give.

Obviously Tahir wasn't the sort to inspire affection.

Far better to be alone and self-contained.

He was stubborn and contemptuous enough never to give in. It was a matter of honour that every time, when it was over, he gathered his strength and walked away. Even if his steps were unsteady and his eyes clouded. Even if he had to haul himself along using furniture or a wall to keep upright.

Sheer willpower always forced him on. He refused to lie broken and cowed at the old Sheikh's feet.

Tahir drew a shaky breath, awake enough to register the constriction in his chest and the pain ripping across his side. Broken ribs?

He couldn't walk away this time. The realisation tore at his pride and ignited his stubbornness.

Something fluttered at his neck. A touch so light that for a moment his dazed brain rejected the notion.

There it was again. Something cool and damp slid from his jaw down his throat, then lower, in a soothing swipe over his chest. And again, from under his chin, the caress edged down, tracing blessed coolness across burning skin.

It stopped and, straining his senses, Tahir heard a splash. A moment later the damp cloth—he was aware enough now to realise what it was—returned, trailing across his pounding forehead and brushing damply at his hair.

He swallowed a moan at the pure pleasure of that cool relief against the searing ache in his head.

Was this some new torture devised by his father? A moment's respite and burgeoning hope to rouse him enough only so he could feel more pain when the beating recommenced?

'Go away.' He moved his lips, worked his throat, but no sound emerged.

The cloth paused, then slid down his cheek in a tender caress that was almost his undoing. He couldn't remember feeling weaker.

His skin burned and prickled, as if stung by a thousand cuts, yet the bliss of that touch made him suck in his breath. That sudden movement scorched his battered torso with a fiery ache.

'Go away.'

He didn't have the strength to withstand the lure of this gentle treatment. It would break him as the pounding fists never could.

'You're awake.' Her voice was a whisper, soft as a soughing breeze. He racked his brain to place it. Surely he couldn't forget a woman with a voice like that? Low and sweet, with a seductive husky edge that set it apart.

He didn't know her. In his foggy brain that fact stood out.

She must be one of his father's women. A new one.

Bitterness flooded his mouth, ousting even the rusty taste of blood. He should have guessed Sheikh Yazan Al'Ramiz would try something new to break his obstinate son. What better than the soft touch of a woman?

'Leave me,' Tahir ordered. But to his shame his voice emerged as a hoarse whisper. Almost a whimper.

'Here.' A firm hand slipped beneath his shoulder and a slim arm supported his skull, lifting him slightly.

Instantly pain shot through him. A stabbing spike of lightning shattered the blankness behind his closed lids and he stiffened against the need to gasp out his agony.

'I know it hurts, but you have to drink.' He heard the voice vaguely, as if through a muffling curtain. Then water, blessedly cool, trickled over his lips. Thought fled as he gulped the precious fluid.

Too soon the flow stopped.

He opened his lips to ask for more, heedless now of pride. But she forestalled him, her voice soothing.

'Be patient. You can have more soon.' She leaned close. He felt her warmth beside and behind him as he lay in her lap. Her scent, wild honey and cinnamon and warm female flesh, teased his nostrils and unravelled his thoughts. 'You're dehydrated. You need fluids, but not too fast.'

'How long before he returns?'

'He?' Her voice was sharp. 'There's no one else. Just you and me.'

Tahir listened to her husky voice, a voice of untrammelled temptation, and suppressed a groan of despair. How could he hold out against the promise of that voice, those gentle hands?

In his weakened state Tahir had no reserves of strength. All he wanted was to have her hold him, nurse him against her undoubtedly soft bosom and pretend there was no such thing as reality.

How long before he begged for the first time in his life?

Damn his father for finally finding a way to break his resistance. She'd sap his willpower as no beating could.

'Tell me.' He struggled to sit higher, but was so weak the press of her palm against his bare chest stopped him. 'When will he be back?'

'Who? Was there someone with you in the desert?' Urgency threaded her voice.

'Desert?' Tahir paused, his brows turning down as he fought to remember. Sheikh Yazan Al'Ramiz enjoyed the luxuries of life too much to spend time in the desert, even if it *was* the traditional home of his forebears.

She was trying to distract him.

'Where is my father?' he whispered through gritted teeth, as pain rose in an engulfing tide. 'He'll want to gloat.'

'I told you, there's no one here but us.'

His face hurt as he grimaced. 'I may have been beaten senseless but I'm not a fool.' He raised a hand and unerringly encircled her wrist where her palm rested against his chest.

She was young, her skin supple and smooth. He felt her pulse race against his fingers, heard her breath catch in the resounding silence that blanketed them.

'Someone *beat* you? I thought you'd been in an accident.'

Finally, against his better judgement, he forced his weighted eyelids open. The world was dark and blurred. It took a long time to focus. When he did his breath seized in his lungs.

Damn the old man. He knew Tahir too well. Knew him better than Tahir knew himself.

She glowed in the wavering light, her smooth almost oval face pale and perfect. Her nose was neat and straight. Her lips formed a cupid's bow that promised pure pleasure. His pulse leapt just from looking at it and, despite his pain, heat coiled in Tahir's belly when she furtively swiped her tongue along her top lip as if nervous.

The slightly square set of her jaw hinted at character and a determination that instantly appealed to Tahir. And her eyes… He could sink into the rich sherry-tinted depths of those wide eyes. They looked guileless, gorgeous, beguiling.

Glossy dark hair framed her face. Not a stiff, sprayed coiffure but soft tresses that had escaped whatever she'd done to pull her hair back.

She looked fresh, without a touch of make-up on her exquisite features. She blinked, eyes widening as she met his gaze, then long lush lashes lowered, screening her expression.

She was the picture of innocent seduction.

His poor battered body stirred feebly.

If he'd had the energy Tahir would have applauded his father's choice. How had he known that façade of innocent allure would weaken his son's resolve more than the wiles of a glamorous, experienced woman?

Tahir remembered the first time he'd fallen for the mirage of sweet, virginal womanhood and scowled. Who'd have thought after all this time he'd still harbour a weakness for that particular fantasy? He'd made it his business to avoid falling for it again.

His hand firmed around hers, feeling the fragility of her bones and the thud of her pulse racing. Her face was calm but her pulse told another story.

Did she fear his father? Had she been coerced?

He grimaced, searching for words to question her. But his

eyes flickered shut as the effort of the last minutes took its toll. His fingers opened and her hand slid away.

'Go! Leave before he hurts you too.' Even to his own ears his words sounded slurred and uneven. Tahir groped for the strength to stay awake.

'Who? Who are you talking about?'

'My father, of course.' Walls of pain rose and pressed close, stifling his words, stealing his consciousness.

Annalisa lowered his head and shoulders to the pillow.

Shock hummed through her.

Looking into his searing blue eyes was like staring at the sun too long. Except watching the sky had never made her feel so edgy or breathless.

Even the sound of his deep voice, a mere whisper of sound from his poor cracked lips, made something unravel in the pit of her stomach.

Belatedly she looked around, past the lamp and the low-burning campfire, towards the dune where he'd appeared.

Had he been attacked? If so, by a stranger or by his father, as he'd claimed? Or was that a figment of a mind confused by head wounds? As well as the gash at his temple Annalisa had found a lump like a pigeon's egg on the back of his skull.

For hours she'd been checking his pupils. Though what she'd do if he had bleeding to the brain she didn't know. She couldn't move him. It would be days before the camel train returned and this part of the country's arid centre was a tele-communications black spot.

Fear sidled down her spine and she shivered. All night she'd told herself she'd cope, doing her best to rehydrate the stranger and lower his temperature.

Now she had more to worry about.

She got to her feet and searched her supplies. Her hand closed around cool metal and she dragged it out.

The pistol was an antique. It had belonged to her mother's father, been presented to Annalisa's father on the day he'd wed. A traditional gift from a traditional man. All the men of Qusay knew how to shoot, just as they knew how to ride, and many still had skills in the old sports of archery and hawking.

Annalisa's father, an outsider, had never used the gun. As a respected doctor he'd never needed to protect himself or his family. But she felt better with it in her hand.

She'd brought it for sentimental reasons, remembering how he'd carried it on their trips into the wilderness.

Once more that dreadful sense of aloneness swept over her, pummelling her stomach and stealing the calm she'd worked so hard to maintain.

What if someone else was out there, lost and injured or angry and violent? She bit her lip, knowing she couldn't search. If she left the oasis her patient would likely die of dehydration and exposure.

She returned to his side. His temperature was too high. She picked up the cloth but was loath to touch him again.

Despite the nicks and abrasions marring his face he was a handsome man. More handsome than any she'd met before. Even with deep purple shadows beneath his eyes and the wound at his temple. Dark stubble accentuated a lean, superbly sculpted countenance. Even his hands, large and strong and sinewed, were strangely fascinating.

Annalisa remembered the feel of his fingers encircling her wrist and wondered at the sensations that had bombarded her. She'd felt wary yet excited.

Her gaze slipped to his bare chest. She'd spread his shirt open to bathe him and try to reduce his fever.

In the mellow light from the lamp and the flickering fire he looked beautiful, despite the bruises marring his firm golden skin. His chest was broad and muscular but not with the pumped-up look she'd seen on men in movies and foreign magazines. His latent strength looked natural but no less formidable for that. As for the way his powerful torso tapered to a narrow waist and hips... Annalisa knew a shameful urge to sit and stare.

Even the fuzz of dark hair across his pectoral muscles looked appealing. She wanted to touch it. Discover if it was soft or coarse against her palm.

Her gaze strayed to the narrowing line of hair that led from his chest down his belly.

Annalisa's pulse hit a discordant beat and staggered on too fast. Heat washed her cheeks and shame burnt as she realised she'd been ogling him.

Determined, she squeezed the cloth, took a fortifying breath and wiped the damp fabric over him.

She refused to think about how her hand shook as it followed the contours of his body, or about the alien tingle in her stomach that signalled a reaction to a man who, even asleep, was more potently virile than any male she'd encountered.

Tahir woke to pain again. At least the throb in his head didn't threaten to take the back off his skull, as it had before. Only one jackhammer was at work there now.

His lips twisted in a rueful smile that felt more like a grimace from scratched, sore lips. He stirred, opening his eyes a fraction. Not darkness. Not bright daylight either. The light filtering through his lashes was green-tinged and shadowed.

He heard the soft stirring of the wind, breathed deep and inhaled the unique scent that was Qusay. Heat and sand and some indefinable hint of spice he'd never been able to identify.

A searing blast of confused feelings struck him, roiling in his gut, rising in his throat.

'I'm not dead, then.' The words, hoarse as they were, sounded loud.

'No, you're not dead.'

His muscles froze as he heard a voice, half remembered. Soft, rich, slightly husky. The voice of a temptress sent to tease a man too weak to resist.

She spoke again, 'You don't seem particularly pleased.'

Tahir shrugged, then stiffened as abused muscles shrieked in protest.

He didn't explain his innermost thoughts to anyone.

'Why is it green? Where are we?' He kept his head averted, preferring not to face the owner of that voice till he had himself in hand. He felt strangely at a loss, unable to summon his composure, as if this last beating had shattered the brittle shell of disdain he used to maintain distance from the brutality around him.

Tahir blinked, amazed at how vulnerable he felt. How weak.

'We're at the Darshoor oasis, in the heart of Qusay's desert.' Her voice slid like rippling water over him and for a moment his hazy mind strayed.

Till her words sank in.

'The desert?' He whipped his head round then shut his eyes as a blast of white-hot pain stabbed him.

'That's right. The light's green because you're in my tent.'

A tent. In the desert. The words whirled in his head but they didn't make sense.

'My father—'

'He's not here.' She broke in before he could cobble his thoughts together. 'You seemed to think he was here too but you're confused. You were…disturbed.'

Tahir frowned. None of this made sense. His father lived in the city, with easy access to his vices of choice: women, gambling and brokering power and money corruptly.

'You seemed to think you'd been beaten.'

Instantly Tahir froze. He would never have admitted such a thing, especially to a stranger! Not even to his closest friends.

Who *was* this woman?

He forced his eyelids open again and found himself sinking into warm sherry-tinted depths.

By daylight she looked even better than she had the first time. For he remembered her now, this woman who'd haunted his thoughts. Or were they dreams?

'Who are you?' A swift glance took in hair scrupulously pulled back from her lovely face, an absence of jewellery, a long-sleeved yellow shirt and beige cotton trousers. She didn't dress like a local in concealing skirts. Yet surely only a local would be here?

From where he lay, looking up, her legs looked endless. She moved and he watched the fabric pull tight over her neatly curved hip and slim thighs. A moment later she sat on the floor beside him, her faint, sweet fragrance tantalising his nostrils. Her shirt pulled across her breasts as she leaned towards him.

A jolt of sensation shot through his belly.

No. He wasn't dead yet.

Perhaps there were some compensations after all.

'My name is Annalisa. Annalisa Hansen.' She paused, as if waiting for him to say something. 'You arrived at my campsite days ago. Just walked out of the desert.'

'Days ago?' How could he have lost so much time?

'You're injured.' She gestured to his head, his side. 'My guess is you were in the desert for quite a while. When you reached me you were seriously dehydrated.' She lifted a hand to his brow. Her palm was cool and curiously familiar.

He had a jumbled recollection of her touching him earlier. Of blessed water and soothing words.

'You've been drifting in and out of consciousness.' She leaned back, lifting her hand away, and Tahir knew a bizarre desire to catch it back.

'Your little friend has been worried.'

'Little friend?' Automatically he looked past her, taking in the cool interior of the tent, the neatly stowed gear in one corner. A ripple of pages as a furtive breeze played across a book left open a few metres away.

'You don't remember?' She surveyed him seriously.

'No.' He remembered just in time not to shake his head. He was no masochist and the pain was already bad enough. 'I don't recall.'

It was true. His thoughts were fluid and incomplete. He was unable to fix anything in his mind.

'That's all right,' she said with the calm air of one who'd perfected a soothing bedside manner. Vaguely he wondered who this woman was, caring for him at a desert oasis. 'You've taken a nasty knock to the head so things could be jumbled for a while.'

'Tell me,' he murmured, forcing down rising concern at his faulty memory. He recalled a casino. A woman all but climbing into his lap as the chips rose before him. He remembered a cruiser in a crowded marina. A party in a city penthouse. A meeting in a hushed boardroom. But the faces were blurred. The details unclear. 'What little friend?'

The woman…Annalisa, he reminded himself…smiled. A shaft of sunlight pierced the interior of the tent, or so it seemed, as he stared up into her calm, sweet face.

'You were carrying a goat.'

'A goat?' What nonsense was this?

'Yes.' This time her smile was more like a grin. Her dark eyes danced and she tilted her head engagingly. 'A little one. Obviously it's a friend of yours. It's been foraging for food but it keeps coming back to sleep just outside the tent.'

A goat? His mind was blank. Frighteningly blank.

'What else?' he murmured. There must be more.

She shrugged and he caught a flash of something in her eyes. Distress? Fear?

'Nothing else. You just appeared.' She waited but he said nothing. 'So, perhaps you could tell me something.' She lifted a hand and tugged nervously at her earlobe. 'Who are you?'

'My name is Tahir…'

'Yes?' She nodded encouragingly.

A sensation like a plummeting lift crashed through the sudden void that was his stomach. Blood rushed in his ears as he met her gaze. The kaleidoscope of blurry images cascaded through his brain into nothingness.

'And I'm afraid that's all I can tell you.'

He forced a smile to lips that felt stiff and unfamiliar. 'I seem to have mislaid my memory.'

CHAPTER THREE

FOR a man who couldn't remember his name Tahir was one cool customer.

Annalisa read the shock flaring in his eyes and the way he instantly masked it. Ready sympathy surged but she beat it down, knowing instinctively he'd reject it.

Despite never having left Qusay, Annalisa had seen a lot in her twenty-five years. As her father's assistant she'd seen the effects of accident and disease, the way pain or fear could break even the strongest will.

Yet this man, traumatised by wounds that must be shockingly painful, smiled at her with a veneer of calm indifference. As if he were one of her father's scientist friends and they were conversing over a cup of sweet tea in her father's study.

Yet none of her father's friends looked like Tahir. Or made her feel that warm tingle of awareness deep inside.

Years ago, with Toby, the man she'd planned to marry, she'd known something like it. But not so instantaneously, nor so strong.

There was something about Tahir that she connected with at the deepest level. More than his extraordinary looks or the innate sophistication that had nothing to do with his beautiful clothes. Something that set him apart. She was drawn by his core of inner strength, revealed as intensely blue eyes met hers with wry humour, ignoring the unspoken fear that his memory lapse was permanent.

He comes from another world. One where you don't belong.

She'd do well to remember it.

A pang shot through her and her calm frayed at the edges. *Just where did she belong?*

All her life she'd never fitted in. She was a Qusani but didn't live as other Qusani women or fit their traditional role. She was poised between two worlds, belonging to neither. She'd been part of her father's world, his assistant, his confidante.

But he'd gone, leaving her bereft.

'What's wrong?' Tahir's deep voice roused her from melancholy reflection. 'Are you all right?'

Despite herself Annalisa smiled. Lying flat on his back, bruised and barely awake, his memory shot, yet this man was concerned for *her*?

She laid a reassuring hand on his arm. His muscles tensed beneath the fine cotton of his shirt. His warm strength radiated up through her fingertips and palm.

A zap of something jagged between them as she met those piercing eyes. His nonchalant half-smile disappeared, replaced by frowning absorption.

'Nothing's wrong,' she said briskly, slipping her hand away. It tingled from the contact and she clenched it at her side. 'Your foggy memory is normal. It should come back in time.' She drew her lips up in a smile she hoped looked reassuring. 'You've got two head wounds. Either would be enough to knock you about for a couple of days.'

Or do far worse. Ruthlessly she pushed aside the fear that he might be more badly injured than she realised.

'You speak as if you have medical experience.'

'My father was a doctor. The only doctor in our region. I helped him for years.' She turned away, horrified by the way memories swamped her again, and the pain with it. 'I don't have medical qualifications but I can set a sprain or treat a fever.'

'Why do I suspect you've done much more than that for me, Annalisa?'

The sound of her name on his lips was strangely intimate. Reluctantly she turned back, meeting his warm gaze, feeling his approval trickle through her like water in a parched landscape.

'You've saved my life, haven't you?' His voice dropped to a low rumble that vibrated along her skin.

Annalisa shrugged, uncomfortable with his praise. Uncomfortable with her intense reaction to this stranger. She'd done all she could but he wasn't out of the woods yet. Fear edged her thoughts.

'You'll be okay, given time.' Fervently she prayed she was right. 'All you need to do is rest and give yourself time to recuperate. And try not to worry.' She'd do enough worrying for the pair of them.

Even now she couldn't quite believe he was holding a sensible conversation. He'd drifted in and out of consciousness since he'd stumbled into her life, leaving her terrified but doggedly determined to do what she could.

'I want to check your reactions.' She moved to kneel at the end of the mattress. 'Can you move your feet?'

She watched as he rotated his ankles and then lifted first one foot then the other. Relief coursed through her.

'Excellent. I'm going to hold your feet. When I tell you, push against my hands. Okay?'

'Okay.'

Gently she lifted his heels onto her knees and cupped his bare feet with her palms. A curious jolt of heat shot through her from the contact. She blinked and tried to concentrate.

His feet were long, strong and well shaped. For a moment she knelt there blankly staring, absorbing the sensation of skin on skin.

She'd never before thought of feet as sexy.

Annalisa's brow puckered. She felt out of her depth.

'Annalisa?' His voice yanked her mind back and heat seared her cheeks. She kept her head bent and concentrated on what her father had said about head injuries.

'Push against my hands.' Instantly she felt steady pressure. She smiled and looked up, meeting his narrowed stare. 'That's good.'

Carefully she lowered his feet and moved up beside him, leaning over so he didn't have to twist to face her.

'Now, take my hands,' she said briskly, adopting a professional manner. But it was hard when eyes like sapphires fixed unblinkingly on her. She wondered what he saw, whether he read her trepidation and uncertainty.

Large hands, powerful but marred by scratches, lifted towards her.

Not allowing herself to hesitate, Annalisa placed her hands in his. She told herself the swirling in her abdomen was relief that he was well enough to cooperate.

'Now, squeeze,' she murmured, ignoring the illusion of intimacy engendered by their linked hands.

Again the pressure was equal on both left and right sides. Her shoulders dropped a fraction as relief surged. For now the signs were good.

She moved to pull back, slide her hands from his. Instantly long fingers twined with hers, holding her still.

Her heart gave a juddering thump as their gazes meshed. She realised how she leaned across him, the heat of his bare torso warming her through the thin fabric of her clothes. The way his eyes flashed with something unidentifiable yet disturbing. Her breathing shortened. She felt vulnerable, though he was the injured one.

'What are you checking?' The words were crisp. Not slurred like when he'd called out in his sleep.

'Just making sure your reactions are normal.' She met his gaze steadily, refusing to mention the possibility of bleeding to the brain. 'They are. You should be up and about in no time.'

'Good. I find I have a burning desire to bathe. You said this is an oasis?'

'Yes, but—'

'Then there's no problem getting water.' He paused. 'I'll need someone from your party to help me get upright.'

'There's only me. And I don't think bathing is a good idea yet.'

His eyes darkened in surprise. 'You're alone?'

She nodded.

'You're a remarkable woman, Annalisa Hansen.' His grip loosened and she found herself free. Belatedly she remembered to straighten so she didn't hover over him.

'Do you do this often? Camp alone in the desert?'

She shook her head. 'This is the first time I've been here alone.' Stupidly her voice wobbled on the last word and his eyes narrowed. Abruptly she looked away.

It was almost six months to the day since her father died. Maybe it was the looming anniversary that sideswiped her, dredging up such grief sometimes she thought she couldn't bear it.

Abruptly he spoke, changing the subject. 'If you knew how much sand I've swallowed you wouldn't begrudge me your help to get clean.' He levered himself up on one elbow, then pushed himself higher to sit, swaying beside her.

He ignored her protests, setting his jaw with a steely determination and clambering stiffly to his knees. Finally she capitulated and helped him, realising she couldn't stop him.

It was only later she remembered the look in his bright eyes as grief had stabbed her out of nowhere.

Had he read her pain and decided to distract her?

No, the idea was absurd.

Tahir cursed himself for being every kind of fool as he sat in the pool and let water slide around his aching body. He'd known moving was a bad idea, but he refused to play the invalid.

Bad enough that his brain wasn't functioning. The more he tried to remember the more the ache in his skull intensified, matching the searing pain in his ribs. He let his thoughts skitter from the possibility the damage was permanent. He wouldn't accept that option.

It made him even more determined to conquer his physical weakness.

Then there was the memory of Annalisa's soft brown eyes, brimming with distress as she avoided his gaze.

Despite her brisk capability he sensed pain, a deep vulnerability. Looking into her shadowed eyes, Tahir had felt an overwhelming need to wipe her hurt away.

Enough to brave getting to his feet.

Fool! He'd almost collapsed. Only her support had kept him upright the few metres to the water. Now he sat waist-deep, naked but for the silk boxers he'd kept on in deference to her presence, wondering how he'd summon the strength to return to the tent.

Wondering how long he could keep his eyes off the woman who sat watchfully beside the stream.

It had been torture of a different sort, allowing her to undress him. Her soft hands fumbling at his trousers had been a torment that had made him forget for a brief moment the pain bombarding him. The sight of her kneeling before him, drawing his trousers off as he leaned on her shoulder, had evoked sensations no invalid should feel.

Then she'd waded into the water, supporting him. She'd been heedless of the way their unsteady progress had sent up sprays of water that soaked large patches of her trousers and shirt.

But Tahir hadn't.

When he shut his eyes he still saw her lace bra outlined against transparent cotton, cupping voluptuous breasts that strained forward as she steadied him. He remembered the neat curve of her hip, the narrow elastic ridge of bikini underwear where her trousers plastered her skin, then the long supple line of her thigh.

Tahir's mouth dried and it had nothing to do with the arid air.

He should be frantically trying to remember who he was. Trying to piece together the fragments of memory, like snippets of disjointed film, swirling in his head.

Instead his thoughts circled back to Annalisa. Who was she? Why was she here?

Despite the cool water, his groin throbbed as he watched her patting a spindly-legged goat.

Was he like this with other women? So easily aroused?

He remembered the woman at the casino. The one in beads and diamonds and little else, who'd been so amorous. The memory didn't spark anything. No heat. No desire.

Tahir frowned. He had an unsettling presentiment he should be very worried by his reactions to Annalisa Hansen.

Bathing in the *wadi* had been a huge mistake. Annalisa bit her lip as Tahir mumbled in his sleep, his dark brows arrowing fiercely in a scowl. These last hours he'd grown unsettled and she'd feared for him, giving up her position by the telescope to sit at his side.

He rolled, one arm outflung, dislodging the blanket and baring his chest to the rapidly cooling night air.

She strove not to think about the fact that he was naked beneath the bedding. He'd barely made it back from bathing when he'd collapsed on the makeshift bed, shucking off his wet boxers with complete disregard for her presence. She doubted he'd even realised she was there.

But to her chagrin she had perfect recall. *Detailed recall.* A blush warmed her throat at the memory of his tightly curved buttocks, heavily muscled thighs and—

'Father!' The hoarse groan yanked her into the present.

Tahir's head thrashed and Annalisa winced, thinking of the lump on his skull.

'Shh. It's all right, Tahir. You're safe.' Whatever nightmares his injuries conjured, they rode him like demons. He sounded desperate.

She leaned across, touching his forehead. His temperature was normal, thank God, but—

A hand snapped around her wrist and dragged it to his side. The movement caught her off balance. She tugged, but the harder she fought, the more implacable his hold, till she leant right across him. His frown deepened, and his firmly sculpted lips moved silently, the muscles of his jaw clenching beneath dark stubble.

He pulled. With an *oof* of escaping air she landed on him. Frantically she tried to find purchase without digging her elbows into his ribs, but his other arm came round her. There was no escape.

'He sent you, didn't he?' The words were a low growl.

'No one sent me.' She tried to slip down out of his grip but he simply lashed his arm tighter round her back, dragging her till she lay over him, her legs sinking between his when he moved.

Heat radiated up from tense muscles and she stiffened. With each breath she was aware of his chest, his hipbones, his thighs like hot steel around her.

'He knew what he was doing, damn him.' Tahir's voice was rough and deep, resonating up from his chest and right through her.

Annalisa struggled to ignore her fascination at being so close, encircled by him. Even with Toby, even when he'd taken her in his arms and talked of a future together, she had never been this close. This…intimate. He'd respected that in Qusay a woman's chastity was no light gift to bestow. He'd promised to wait. Except their bright future had never eventuated.

'Houri…' Tahir mumbled, and his searing breath feathered her scalp. Tremors ran down her spine and spread in slow-turning circles through her belly. 'Temptress.'

His grip eased and he smoothed a hand down her back. It felt so good she fought not to arch into his touch, like a cat responding to a caress. Spread across him, in full-length contact as he stroked her and murmured in her ear, Annalisa felt an unravelling in the pit of her stomach. A heat that was unfamiliar and edgy and worrying.

His hand moulded her buttocks, dragging her closer. The unmistakable ridge of male arousal against the apex of her thighs grew pronounced and she bit her lip as his caress rubbed her against it.

He didn't know what he was doing. Yet the pulse building between her legs and the heat there proved that didn't matter. She shuddered in horrified excitement at her own arousal.

Who'd known a man's body could feel so very good?

'Mustn't…' His voice died as his hands stopped their trawling caress. He drew a shuddering breath that pushed his chest to her breasts. Annalisa shut her eyes, willing herself not to react even as her nipples peaked in delight.

She waited a few moments then tried to ease away. Instantly his embrace hardened, imprisoning her.

Tahir grew quiet, his mutterings less vehement.

Annalisa waited ten minutes then tried again. Even in sleep Tahir held her tight, refusing to release her.

Telling herself she had no choice but to bide her time till he was completely relaxed, she gave up the unequal struggle to hold herself even marginally away. Her head sagged and her muscles went limp as she sank into him. She was going nowhere yet.

* * *

A shaft of early-morning light woke Tahir. Instantly the familiar low-grade hum of abused muscles, torn flesh and a battered head roused him to full wakefulness.

And something else. Sexual awareness.

More than awareness. Delight drenched him as he absorbed the full extent of his good fortune.

He lay on his side with Annalisa in his embrace. Her head was on his arm, her knees bent, allowing his bare legs to spoon in behind her. He breathed deep and the sweet fragrance of her hair filled his nostrils, shimmering there like a promise of pleasures to come. She was warm and curved, slim but rounded, exactly where it counted.

Not daring to breathe, Tahir gently flexed his fingers, cupping the exquisite ripeness of her breast. He'd pushed her shirt aside and her bra was soft, a thin layer of lace between his fingers and her feminine bounty.

His breath whistled out from contracting lungs and he cursed silently, not ready yet for her to wake and move away. It was clear that whatever had led to them sharing the narrow mattress, it wasn't sex. Annalisa was fully clothed.

But clothes provided little protection. Not when he lay flush against her.

He shut his eyes, realising exactly how aroused he was. The sweet curve of her buttocks pressed against him in unconscious invitation. Her warmth enclosed him and he fought rising lust. Fought the need to thrust against her and appease the hunger eating at his belly. Or better yet, to tear those light trousers away and bury himself deep within her pliant, lush body.

Pain shot through him and Tahir realised he'd locked his jaw so tight it felt as if he might dislocate it.

Slowly he breathed, telling himself to move. He had no right to hold her like this. But he wanted…how badly he wanted her.

For long minutes he lay, tense and still, his instincts at war. His palm pressed against her breast and he couldn't help tightening his grip, his fingers encircling her budding nipple.

Was this the sort of man he was? To take advantage of a

sleeping woman? A woman who'd shown him nothing but kindness and not a hint of sexual interest?

His breath shuddered out, riffling her dark unbound hair.

He didn't even know if he was married. Committed to a woman far away and worried about him.

The notion sliced like ice-cold steel through the searing heat of sexual excitement. Moments later he slid away, drawing back carefully so as not to wake her.

Every movement was torment.

The sun was high when Annalisa woke.

She remembered Tahir holding her with a strength that belied his injuries. Remembered realising she needed to wait till his nightmare subsided before escaping.

She recalled the unfamiliar but unmistakable response of her body to Tahir's embrace. Her skin flushed all over as she remembered how she'd revelled in his hardness, his masculine power, even the musky spice scent of his freshly washed skin.

Hastily she tugged her shirt closed, grateful he wasn't there to see how it had come undone during the night.

She suppressed panic that he wasn't there. Surely that was a good sign—that he had enough energy to get up without assistance.

Nevertheless she didn't linger. Despite his strength and his formidable determination he was far from well.

She saw him immediately she left the tent.

He sat with his back against a palm tree, long legs outstretched. He wore the trousers she'd washed and set aside for him. He wasn't naked, as when he'd clasped her close. Yet Annalisa shivered as awareness trickled through her middle, igniting a scorching heat.

Memories of last night and her burgeoning physical responses swamped her. Guilt rose that she'd reacted so to a man who was vulnerable and in her care.

And confusion. In twenty-five years she'd never responded so to any other man.

With his broad bared chest and shoeless feet he looked

untamed, elemental, despite his tailored dress trousers. Annalisa recalled the texture of that fine fabric. Even to her untutored touch she knew it to be of finest quality. Proof that Tahir came from a place far beyond here. That he belonged in another milieu.

Yet, sitting with the sunlight glancing off the golden skin of his straight shoulders, he looked at home. Like a rakish marauder taking his ease. Only the bruises mottling his ribs and the gash at his temple belied the image.

She followed the play of muscles across his chest as he leaned sideways. Annalisa tried and failed to ignore a disturbing new sensation deep in her abdomen.

It felt curiously like hunger.

'Here.' He hadn't noticed her, but spoke instead to the tiny goat he'd carried into the oasis. It stood beside him, stretching up towards a scanty green bush. Tahir reached out an arm and drew a slender branch low enough for the animal to reach.

She didn't know another man who'd bother. Here in Qusay, except for prized horses, animals weren't cosseted.

Despite his outrageously potent masculinity, there was a softer side to him.

Had she imagined Tahir's motives last night? She'd been almost convinced part of his abrupt determination to wash was because he'd seen the stupid tears misting her eyes when she thought of her father. Could he really have sought to divert her thoughts?

It seemed ludicrous, and yet...

'Ah, Sleeping Beauty awakes.' Eyes bright as the morning sun gleamed under straight dark brows. With his burnished skin and black-as-midnight hair those light eyes should have looked wrong somehow.

Yet Annalisa knew with a sinking certainty, as her pulse sped, that she'd never seen a more handsome man. His half-smile drove a deep crease up one lean cheek and her gaze fixed on it with an intensity that appalled her.

'I hope you didn't need me earlier,' she murmured. 'I can't imagine why I overslept.'

'Can't you?' This time he smiled fully, and Annalisa reached out to grab the tent post as her heart kicked and her knees loosened.

What was happening to her?

All her life she'd been sensible, responsible, dutiful. Never, not even on the brink of marriage, had she been swept away by the sheer presence of a man.

'From the little I recall I'd guess you've been running yourself ragged caring for me.'

Annalisa blinked and made herself move from the tent. It felt absurdly as if she was stepping away from safety. But the only danger lay in her reckless response to those piercing blue eyes.

'I packed up your telescope, by the way.'

Swiftly Annalisa turned to the place where her father's telescope had been last night. The location hadn't been ideal, close to the lights of the camp, but she hadn't liked to move too far away in case Tahir needed her.

Swiftly she knelt to undo the battered case.

'Thank you,' she murmured, frantically trying to remember whether she'd covered the lens before going last night to sit with Tahir through his nightmare. If the wind had risen and blasted sand across the lens—

'It seemed okay when I packed it up.'

He was right. There was no damage. Relieved, she sank back on her heels. 'You know about telescopes?'

He shrugged. Unwillingly Annalisa followed the fluid movement of his shoulders.

'Who knows?' His lazy smile slipped and for a moment he looked grim, his eyes cooling to an icy blue.

'I'm sorry.' How could she be so clumsy? 'I'm sure you'll remember soon.' Impulsively she stood and walked towards him, only to stop at his side, self-conscious.

'No doubt you're right.' His easy smile belied the gravity of his expression. 'Sit with me?'

Wordlessly she complied, settling out of arm's reach.

'I remember some things,' he said. 'More than before.'

'Really? That's fantastic. What do you recall?' If he noticed her too-bright tone he said nothing. She'd spent days wondering who he was and how he'd got here. How much worse for him not to know?

Again that shrug. Annalisa slid her gaze from the play of muscle and tanned skin, forcing her breathing to slow.

'Just vague images. A party. Lots of people, but no faces. Places I can't identify.' He paused. 'And a sandstorm, big enough to block the light.'

She nodded. 'That was just before I came out here.'

'I remember the vastness of the desert.' His eyes snared hers. 'Which leads me to wonder how we get out of here and if you've got enough food to keep us both in the meantime.'

'There's plenty.' Out of habit she'd catered for two. 'As for transport, there's a camel route through the oasis.'

'And a camel train is coming back soon?'

Annalisa's bright smile faded. 'Not straight away. In a few days.'

She'd prayed they'd return early and take Tahir to hospital. Now her desperation was edged with other emotions.

'A few more days?' he repeated. 'Maybe more?' His voice was disturbingly deep, his scrutiny so intense it was like a touch, and Annalisa sucked in a quick breath.

'You and me, alone in the desert.'

She met his unreadable eyes. Her stomach dipped. She lifted her chin, battling emotions she didn't understand.

Last night's intimacy had changed everything.

For the first time their enforced solitude felt…dangerous.

CHAPTER FOUR

ANNALISA needn't have worried. Even now he was up and about Tahir didn't encroach on her personal space. If anything he seemed to prefer distance. The idea stabbed her with ridiculous regret.

Occasionally she caught a look, a blaze of azure fire from under half-lowered lids, that stole her breath and set her pulse racing. But she knew it was imagination, her own guilty craving.

The only danger came from her wayward thoughts. They drew blushes to her cheeks and brought a twist of awareness deep inside her.

Meanwhile she was forced to keep an eye on him. Annalisa thought he was out of danger, but he still slept a lot and occasionally his temperature spiked worryingly. Nor could he recall more than disjointed images.

She almost wished she'd followed her father's urgings and studied medicine. Then she'd know what to do. But, though she'd been proud to act as her dad's assistant, medicine wasn't her dream.

'How long have you been an astronomer?'

Annalisa's gaze jerked up from the meal she was preparing over the fire. Tahir sat in his usual place by the palm tree, reading in the fading light—one of the astronomy books she'd brought.

The question was innocuous. But it struck her that this was the first time he'd asked anything personal. His questions were always about the desert and Qusay. She'd enjoyed their discussions and his quick intelligence. She wasn't used to talking about herself.

'I'm not an astronomer. But my father was an amateur one. I grew up looking at the stars.'

Tahir tilted his head consideringly. 'It's your father who usually comes into the desert with you?'

She busied herself lifting the pan from the fire. 'That's right.' Those treks had been special, precious time out from her father's busy practice.

'But he couldn't come this time?'

She forced herself to concentrate on dishing up the couscous flavoured with nuts, spices and dried fruits.

'My father is dead.' It sounded bald, almost aggressive. But Annalisa found it hard to speak of him. He'd been the centre of her life, her mainstay and friend.

'I'm sorry for your loss, Annalisa.' The simple words flowed like soothing balm over raw-edged nerves, at odds with the shivery excitement evoked by the rare sound of her name on Tahir's lips.

'Thank you.' She paused, feeling she should say more. 'It's been six months but still it's hard.'

'And you have no one else?'

Her shoulders stiffened. His words reminded her too much of her family's urgings for her to marry. They meant well, but it grew increasingly difficult to avoid their offers to arrange a marriage to a respectable man who'd take care of her.

She'd grown up with all the freedoms her father had taken for granted with his foreign background. Even her dear, traditional grandfather had understood an arranged marriage wouldn't work for her. She'd be stifled, living the more restricted life of a traditional Qusani wife.

But her grandfather was gone, like her dad. Her lips tightened as grief hollowed her chest.

She didn't need taking care of. Instead she had plans to see the world she'd only heard about. The places her father and his friends had spoken of. To build her own life.

'My mother died when I was young. But I'm not alone.' She smiled ruefully as she ladled their food. 'I have aunts and uncles, cousins and their children.' She was a cuckoo in her mother's family, never quite fitting in.

'Thank you.' Tahir took a plate from her hands and sat with easy grace beside her. 'So how did a doctor called Hansen come to be in Qusay? It's not a local name.'

'It's Danish.' Annalisa sat on the matting, overly conscious of the big man so near. 'My father was half-Danish, half-English. He came here years ago to look at the stars. He loved the place and decided to stay.'

She didn't add the old family story about him taking one look at Annalisa's mother and falling in love on the spot. How she'd loved him at first sight too and they'd waited years for family approval before marrying.

'So you're carrying on a family tradition with your star-gazing?' She caught his bright stare and felt absurdly as if she were falling. It unnerved her.

'Sort of. My father believed he'd found a comet. He and various friends around the world hoped to prove its existence.' She dragged in an uneven breath, remembering the promise she'd given to her father. 'I'm hoping to see it. The Asiya Comet.'

'Nice name.'

She nodded, swallowing hard. Her mother's name. She barely remembered her mother. It was her father's grief she recalled, and his love, steady after all those years. He'd fought debilitating illness to live long enough to prove the comet existed and name it. His body had failed before he'd got to see it himself.

Annalisa blinked to clear her vision. 'I promised I'd be here to see it.' One last pilgrimage before she left.

Scientists around the globe were looking out for the comet this week. She'd be here in Qusay, her mother's home, to watch it for her father.

'Tonight?' At her startled look he gestured to the meal she'd prepared. 'We're eating earlier than usual.'

Annalisa nodded abruptly, reminded again of how much this man of few words noticed.

Had he also noticed the way her gaze followed him? Hastily she looked away, unnerved by the bewildering feelings that plagued her.

'All being well, yes.' She breathed deep.

'Then what will you do?' His voice was soft, like silk brushing her skin. 'Once you've seen your comet?'

Annalisa pushed aside her nervousness at what came next. It was what she wanted, what she'd always planned.

'Then I leave Qusay.' Even saying the words it didn't seem real. After years of wanting to see the wider world, suddenly the time was here. 'I'm going to travel, for a few months at least. Meet the scientists my father and I have corresponded with for so long. Play tourist.' She smiled as she imagined herself in Copenhagen, Rome, Paris. 'Then I'm going to university.'

'Medicine or astronomy?'

'Neither. This time I'm following my own star. I'm going to be a teacher.'

Tahir paced, so restless tonight he couldn't settle. His skin was too tight, his senses on edge, his head throbbing. He told himself it was impatience with his slow recovery, with his scattered memory.

But he knew the cause lay elsewhere. *With Annalisa.*

He'd kept to himself as much as he could. But thrown together as they were in one campsite, one tent, distance didn't account for much. Especially when he only had to close his eyes to see the sweet curve of her lips, the delicious bounty of her breasts and hips.

The scent of her skin, sweet as honey, wafted on the very air. The sound of her voice, soft and throaty, made him aware of her femininity and his own masculine need for her.

Yet it wasn't her exquisite body alone that made his blood hum. There was some indefinable quality that tugged at him. Her calm, capable demeanour, so at odds with that seductress's mouth. Her gentle touch. Her quick mind. And the intensity of her pleasure: when she'd laughed at the antics of the unkempt goat that still hung around the campsite, or tonight when she'd spoken of travelling. Her whole heart shone in her smile and Tahir basked in its radiance. More than anything he wanted her to turn that smile on him.

He picked up his pace, plunging into the darkness at the far end of the oasis where the shrubs grew thick.

Too late he realised his mistake, as his eyes widened and his libido roared into unfettered overdrive.

The sound of splashing reached his ears just as he saw moonlight silver a sinuous form in the stream. A form that was all lush curves and elegant lines. A figure that would make a man get down on bended knee and plead for the privilege of simply stroking that satiny skin.

Only the belief that he was sleeping off another bout of fatigue would have tempted Annalisa into total nudity.

Tahir sent up silent thanks for his wakefulness.

His gaze slipped hungrily along her body, traced the evocative darkness at the juncture of her thighs, dwelt on the supple twist of her spine.

She lifted her hands to smooth water off her hair and the movement raised her breasts invitingly high.

The impact of the sight was like a series of juddering implosions through his body. Arousal was instantaneous. Heat speared him as every muscle hardened. His breathing was an uneven rasp, his hands clenching desperately at his sides.

So focused was he on reining in the need to reach for her that it took a moment for his brain to kick into gear.

To realise he'd seen her like this before.

She'd stood gloriously naked in the afternoon light, like a nymph, perfect, sweet and utterly seductive in this very stream.

He put a hand to his head as the stars wheeled above him. The scattered images in his mind took on a sharp new clarity.

Staggering over that sand dune to the oasis, a warm weight in his arms.

Lying in the sun, his mouth as dry as the great Qusani desert.

His pleasure at the dangerous game of low flying over the sandhills.

Ragged shreds, but enough to give him a sense of identity.

* * *

'You see it?' Annalisa's voice rose in excitement. Soon the comet would disappear, but for now its tail was clear. 'My father was right.' Pride rose, curving her lips.

'I see it.'

Tahir sounded subdued as he bent over the telescope. He'd been that way since he'd emerged from the tent a short time ago. Annalisa hadn't liked to wake him, knowing how important it was that he rested. But finally he'd emerged and picked his way through the unlit campsite to where she'd stood by the telescope. The way he'd moved, with a sure, cat-like grace, had distracted her from the comet.

But she was glad he'd come. Glad there was someone with whom to share the moment. Glad it was Tahir.

He lifted his head and she felt his scrutiny.

'Congratulations. You must be very proud.' He paused and shoved a hand back through his hair. The moonlight showed it rumpled and far too appealing.

Annalisa pulled her jacket tighter, telling herself it was the chill desert night that made her skin prickle, not the insane desire to copy his movements and furrow her own hand through his thick hair.

She forced herself to turn back to the starry sky. 'It's marvellous, isn't it? Now it will be officially recorded, just as he wanted.'

Side by side they watched the comet track towards the horizon. To the naked eye it was just visible.

When it was gone they stood a moment longer, alone in the vast silence. Then Annalisa began to dismantle the telescope.

Emotions flooded her, too many to name. But as she worked on her father's precious equipment she realised that rising above them all was a sense of loss. Her fingers faltered at the task she'd done countless times. Her breath hitched.

Since her father's death she'd focused on this night. On fulfilling his dying wish.

Now it was done. Time to move on. Yet suddenly her plans for the future seemed insignificant in the face of the emptiness engulfing her.

She felt…bereft. Her father truly was gone. Her past life, so busy and organised and full, was over.

The future yawned before her like a dark void. A shudder ripped through her.

'Here,' said a warm voice in her ear. 'I'll finish, if you trust me.'

Annalisa watched his deft movements. How easily he stowed the telescope and hoisted the case, leading the way to the tent.

'Just like that and it's all over.' Her voice sounded stretched and brittle.

'Until the next time Asiya passes by.'

'Of course.' She entered the tent and fumbled inside for the lantern.

It was ridiculous to feel this way. Her grief seemed as fresh as on the day her father had died. She pursed her lips, striving to conquer the raw pain of loss.

She had everything to look forward to. Travel. A career. New friends. New experiences.

Yet at this moment she felt so alone.

Finally the lamp glowed reassuringly. She turned away, only to find Tahir unexpectedly close, his warmth enveloping her.

Their eyes met and held.

'Ah, Annalisa, don't weep.' His hoarse whisper scraped across her skin.

'I'm not—' Her words stopped as he reached out and brushed her cheek. Hard, calloused fingers against wet flesh.

Amazement froze her.

She didn't cry. She had no time for tears.

Though her father was gone the locals still came to her for advice. It was she who'd reassured them. Who'd lobbied for a doctor to replace her father. Who'd taken the new medic to meet the community and help build acceptance for him. Who'd ensured her father's comet got official recognition.

Now it was all done and she was no longer needed.

She felt…adrift.

Horrified at her weakness, she stared up into eyes as clear and pure as those alpine streams she'd dreamed of seeing for herself. Tahir's brows furrowed as if in concentration while his long fingers smoothed her cheek.

She swayed forward to the rhythm of his touch then, startled, drew back.

Dark lashes veiled his eyes. His face was expressionless, still, waiting. He cupped her jaw and the pulse beneath her chin throbbed against his touch.

'You should be proud,' he murmured. 'And happy.'

'I am.' She fought back a self-pitying sniff. She was stronger than this. Her sudden weakness was inexplicable.

'You miss him.' He paused, letting the silence lengthen. 'It's difficult being alone, but you're strong. You'll survive.' The words were whisper-soft, barely audible. Yet the timbre of his voice, like a desert zephyr at daybreak, heralded something new.

More than just pity. Understanding. A precious sense that she wasn't alone. That he knew all she felt.

Abruptly Tahir dropped his hand and stepped back.

The distance between them made her shiver anew. Instinctively she moved forward, only to halt as his eyes blazed with sudden heat.

Ever since falling asleep in his arms Annalisa had known this man was dangerous in ways she barely comprehended. But she'd shoved that knowledge aside, trying to be grateful when he kept his distance.

Now, reading the glittering hunger in his eyes, she knew a reckless desire to walk straight into danger.

Not giving herself time to think, letting instinct drive her, she stepped close, lifting her hand to the hard line of his jaw.

Sensation shot through her as her sensitive palm scraped his shadowed chin. His days-old growth of beard tickled and teased. Darts of fire scorched through her, making her belly cramp and her legs quake.

His mouth firmed to a severe line and he drew a slow breath. Did he too notice the suddenly heavy scent of musk and heat on the night air? His hand clamped hers.

'You're not thinking straight.' His words were harsh and she read tension in his shoulders.

'Please, Tahir.' She didn't know what she pleaded for, yet she knew she couldn't bear him to turn away.

'What is it you want, Annalisa?' His deep voice sounded strained and his pulse hammered beneath her touch. That reminder of his vulnerability gave her the courage to meet his gaze head-on.

Mutely she shook her head, unsure how to answer, yet sure she needed *something* from him. Just the warmth of his living skin against hers was balm to a heart that hadn't been allowed time for grief.

The sense of connection felt so real, so profound, she couldn't turn away.

Annalisa raised her other palm and pressed it against the lapel of his dark jacket, absorbing the rhythmic thud of his heart against her hand. So strong. So alive.

'Annalisa.' His deep voice turned gruff with warning—or displeasure. 'Don't.'

Yet he didn't move away. He held her gaze with glittering eyes half-veiled by long lashes that somehow emphasised his utterly masculine features.

'Please...' It was a whisper of sound as she raised herself on tiptoe so her breath feathered his neck, his chin. His warmth enfolded her, drew her.

This near, his mouth was an implacable line, his jaw a study in tension, but the compulsion to touch him, as a woman touched a man, was too strong.

Just this once.

Her eyes flickered shut as she pressed her lips to his. His mouth was soft. Surprised, she pushed closer, enjoying the slight friction as her lips slid along his, revelling in the tickle of stubble against her cheek. She felt daring and powerful and anything but lonely.

She pulled back and opened heavy lids. Her breathing had quickened—or was that his? Their bodies touched in intriguing ways she wanted to explore.

But, looking into his tense face with its brooding angles, Annalisa realised she'd overstepped the mark.

The fluttering excitement in her chest died and her stomach plunged. Heat scalded her cheeks and she looked down at the lapel of his tuxedo.

Some tiny part of her mind told her if she lived to be a hundred she'd never see a man look so good in formal attire. But mostly she just wanted the earth to open and swallow her whole.

She bit her lip, an apology trembling on her tongue. Kissing a man wasn't as easy at it seemed. Especially when he hadn't invited a kiss.

Hastily she stepped back, only to find her way blocked. An arm like iron barred her way.

Startled, she raised her head. His face was set in grim lines yet the burning heat was back in his eyes.

'Is this what you want?' He dipped his head so the words feathered her lips.

Without giving her time to respond, he slanted his mouth across hers. His lips moved, caressed and stroked, and bliss reverberated through Annalisa's body. She trembled and sank against him.

Her hands slipped up to hang on to his broad shoulders, lest she collapse. She felt as if she was falling.

His tongue slicked her bottom lip and she drew a surprised breath. Before she realised what he intended Tahir was stroking the inside of her mouth.

Startled, she stiffened. Then her muscles went lax as he caressed her tongue, inviting her to meet him kiss for kiss.

Tentatively she responded, and was rewarded with a throaty grumble of approval like the purr of a sleepy lion. His other arm lashed round her, drawing her in as he delved deep, leaning over her as if he couldn't get close enough. As if needing to dominate and protect.

The idea thrilled and terrified her.

Powerful thighs surrounded her legs as he tucked her close. Her mind whirled in overload at the intimacy of being held like this. Of sharing a sensual kiss that shattered the boundaries of her experience.

A dull throb pulsed in her stomach and she shifted to ease

it. The movement brought her in contact with Tahir's pelvis and a telltale hardness.

A quiver rocked his body and he hauled her nearer.

Annalisa gasped. Not with shock or disgust.

With delight.

It was all she could do not to slide forward against that exciting bulge.

What sort of wanton had she become?

She was panting, her chest heaving, when he broke the kiss and straightened. His eyes were narrowed slits she couldn't read. But she had no trouble reading the rapid tattoo of the pulse in his neck. It mirrored hers.

Did he feel like this? All warm and jittery and lax? Trembling and dazed and hungry for more?

If anything he looked more in control than ever. His face was as still as a wooden mask. His body rigid but for the rapid rise and fall of his chest.

'Tahir?' She slid a hand from his shoulder up the side of his neck, cupping hot skin. Pleasure skittered through her at that simple contact.

His eyes flickered shut and he bit back a sound that could have been a groan. Instantly she was alert.

'Did I hurt you? Are you in pain?' What had she done? Her hands skimmed the back of his skull, his temple, then down over his wide shoulders. 'Where does it hurt?'

Suddenly she found both hands clasped together in his. Still he didn't open his eyes.

His head was thrown back and she watched the long burnished column of his throat as he swallowed hard.

'Tahir!' Panic edged her voice. 'What's wrong?'

His lips quirked up in the half-smile that always melted her insides. A long crease furrowed his cheek. She wanted to press her lips against it and taste his skin.

'Nothing's wrong, little one.' He looked at her now and his expression held her immobile. Her breath jammed in her throat. 'You didn't answer. Is that what you wanted?'

Jerkily she nodded, eyes fixed on his.

'Say it, Annalisa.' His voice was harsh, but somehow she knew it wasn't anger or disgust that roughened his words. It was the same ribbon of excitement that threaded her body, drawing each muscle and sinew tight.

'I want you to kiss me,' she whispered, spellbound by what she saw in his eyes.

'Is that all?' He leaned forward and she felt his words, small puffs of breath on her ear. She shuddered and his hands firmed around hers. Surprised, she realised they were unsteady. 'What else do you want?'

'I…' How could he ask questions? She didn't want to think and talk. Just wanted to feel.

'Is it this?'

Long fingers brushed the bare skin of her neck, trailing down to the V of her shirt.

Her breath snagged as she willed him to continue. Was that a flicker in his darkening gaze?

Finally his hand slid down, skimming the fabric of her shirt till his palm warmed her breast. She almost cried with frustration as he stood, watching her, almost, *almost* touching her as she wanted, *needed* to be touched.

It rose in her like a tide—a yearning she didn't fully understand, a craving for more, much more.

Annalisa pushed forward into his waiting palm.

His hand closed convulsively around her. It was bliss. It was more than she'd thought possible. Her breath sighed out as he rubbed his thumb over her burgeoning nipple.

Instantly heat jolted through her, right down to her belly. Lower. Where it felt as if she melted.

'Please, Tahir.'

He shook his head, a single jerky movement. 'You need to tell me.' His voice was raw and uneven, as if he held on to control by a thread. 'You want me to touch you like this?' His palm circled and pressed and her knees gave way.

Abruptly his hands closed on her arms, tight enough to hold her steady.

'Annalisa.' Just the sound of him saying her name was too much pleasure to bear. 'We should stop now.'

'No!' She wrenched herself from his hold and plastered herself against his tall frame, no thought now of shyness or distance.

'I don't want to stop. I want…everything, Tahir.' She drew a shuddering breath and forced herself to think of the words, not just the sensations. 'I need you. Please.'

CHAPTER FIVE

THE words were barely out when strong arms brought her down on the bed. Tahir's lips met hers as he peeled her clothes away.

The heat of his body against hers and the fervour of his kisses incited a heady recklessness that didn't allow second thoughts.

Annalisa wanted him so urgently; her need was overwhelming. She shuddered with the force of it as she helped him with clumsy fingers.

Then cool air caressed her skin. Tahir sat back on his heels. His eyes glowed, devouring her in a way that sent flickers of fire racing through her body. He was so intent. Utterly absorbed. Like a hungry man sighting a banquet laid out just for him. Her heart leapt against her ribs.

Annalisa reached for his shirt, needing him close. That scorching scrutiny made her feel vulnerable as never before. She was excited yet nervous, desperate for Tahir but not wanting time to examine what was happening.

For once she wanted to *feel*, not think.

'No.' He clamped his fingers around her hand. 'Not yet. Let me look at you first.'

His trawling gaze moved across her naked breasts, her waist and thighs. It should have made her ashamed or indignant. Qusani women were modest and demure. Annalisa had always thought in that at least she was like her peers.

Now she discovered potent proof that she was different.

Instead of feeling disgust she was *excited* by the flare of lust in Tahir's gaze. She revelled in his unsteady breathing, the pulse throbbing in his neck, and wondered at the reckless woman she'd become.

'Take your hair down.' His whisper grated over her nerves.

Obediently, not taking her eyes from his, she raised her hands to the pins securing her hair. She fumbled, all thumbs, and his gaze dipped to her breasts.

Annalisa barely had time to register the tumble of long tresses on bare skin before Tahir was over her, pushing her into the narrow bed with his body. Solid thighs tangled with hers, the fine weave of his suit slid against her bare flesh and she'd never felt anything so wonderful.

She trembled in delight tinged with anxiety, realising she was utterly in his power.

Then his hands cupped her breasts and he lowered his head. Every nerve in her body centred on that exquisite point of contact.

He touched her nipple with his tongue and she froze. He opened his lips over her areola and she sank into indescribable pleasure, clasping him to her. He settled closer, the unfamiliar weight of his body, his potent masculinity, anchoring her to the mattress.

He suckled, gently at first, then more strongly, and Annalisa cried out in shocked delight, arching convulsively. Her body zinged and sparked with sensations she'd never felt.

How had she lived so long without this? Without him?

'Tahir,' she gasped, 'don't stop.'

With the words Tahir's restraint shattered. His hands roved ceaselessly. He skimmed, stroked and teased till her cries of pleasure grew hoarse. He touched her everywhere, nuzzled the back of her knees, kissed her inner elbow, even sucked her fingers, till it seemed there wasn't one part of her body that didn't sing out with need for him.

She'd never realised physical love could be so consuming. Maybe, if she had time to think, she'd be scared by this intensity. But Tahir didn't permit her time to question.

Restlessly Annalisa shifted, barely noticing the way her

thighs opened wider, letting him sink the full weight of his lower body against her.

What she felt there, the long, solid proof of his virility, made her blood pump faster even as shock filled her. This was *real*, unfamiliar yet compelling.

Gently he bit her ear and her body softened, her breath sighing out.

She responded to Tahir's touch with an eagerness that left her light-headed. Her fingers dug into the soft fabric of his clothes with growing desperation.

She wanted…more.

Whether he sensed it or whether she'd cried it aloud Annalisa didn't know, but finally Tahir let her undo his shirt. Or begin to. Halfway down her hands clenched uselessly against the fine cotton, when his hand arrowed between them, touching her intimately.

Her gaze clung to his heavy-lidded eyes as long fingers slipped to a place no man had touched. The light brush against one tiny, sensitive bud made her whole body jerk as if from an electric shock. A blush seared her throat and cheeks as he watched her.

Part of her wondered at her boldness, letting him caress her so. Yet she couldn't deny her need for him.

His touch circled and there it was again. Unmistakable. High-voltage pleasure at his lightest caress.

She heard her breath loud in her ears, felt her ribcage expand with the desperate need to draw oxygen.

Her breath whooshed out as his touch moved down and into slick heat. Without conscious thought she clamped her muscles around that tiny invasion.

For what seemed for ever Annalisa hung suspended, aware only of the pleasure of his caress and the grim stillness of his face. Tahir looked as if he concentrated every effort on control.

His hand moved fractionally, building a gentle rhythm: along, down, in. And back. And with each stroke she felt herself slip further from the rational world.

She might have no direct experience to draw on but Annalisa

understood what her body told her. What Tahir was doing, the pleasure his caress promised.

Her voice was a raw gasp when it finally emerged. 'No, Tahir. Stop.'

For a moment it seemed he didn't hear. Her body was moving against his touch, her hips rising when his probing fingers stilled. Annalisa bit down a cry of disappointment, her body still throbbing to the beat of his making.

'No?' The single syllable sounded strangled, so foreign she barely recognised it.

'Not like this.' She lifted a shaky hand to his shirt, but was too unsteady to grapple with buttons. 'I want you, not…'

Her words petered out under the weight of sudden shyness and the incendiary flare in his eyes. They blazed like burning sapphires.

Before she had time to gather her thoughts he was gone, rolling off the bed to stand on the matting.

Her instant protest died in her throat as he ripped open his shirt, shrugging out of it and his jacket in one rapid movement. Before she could catch her breath he'd discarded the rest of his clothes.

Breathing became impossible.

Despite the bruises and cuts marring the symmetry of his body, Tahir was the most beautiful being she'd seen.

He moved, and the lamplight caught a line of old scar tissue low on his back. Then he turned and Annalisa's mind atrophied. She'd never seen a naked aroused man. She'd never known one could look so magnificent. Wonderful and slightly frightening at the same time.

He didn't give her time to think. Tahir lowered himself, his bare flesh against hers, hotter than fire. His thighs rubbed hers; the soft hair on his chest abraded her nipples. She welcomed the weight of him pressing her down, took his roughened jaw in her hands and planted a fervent, clumsy kiss against his lips.

A deep rumbling growl vibrated through his chest. Teeth scraped the sensitive skin at her neck and she arched, burying her fingers in the rough silk of his hair. Then she felt pressure where he'd caressed so intimately. Tahir shifted his weight, pushing her legs wide.

She stiffened and the caress at her neck became a tender bite, sending lush waves of pleasure through her. At the same time Tahir moved, pushing up in a slow surge of power.

Pleasure splintered as a ripple of something like pain shot through her, a stinging discomfort that made her catch her breath and stiffen in his hold.

But before she did more than register the sensation Tahir withdrew, lowering his mouth to her breast and laving it until she shivered with renewed desire. She held him near, overwhelmed by the emotions stirring as she watched him, felt him.

When he pressed close again Annalisa rose to him. The feel of his big body against hers held a magic she couldn't resist. Urged by large hands at her thighs she lifted her legs, clasping him close, revelling in the feel of his hot satiny skin.

He raised his head, eyes meeting hers.

There was movement, that bombarding of curious new sensations, and through it all his gaze didn't waver. It held her steady and safe, connected in a way that made her heart swell in her breast as their bodies joined.

This time there was no pain as he pushed deep.

Her body opened to his as if it was meant to be.

He stilled.

There was no sound except a riffle of night breeze against the tent flap and the discreet chirrup of an insect down by the *wadi*. Annalisa didn't breathe. Nor did Tahir. The moment stretched long and portentous between them.

Their gazes meshed as she absorbed the full weight of what they'd done. She read the grim tension drawing his lean features. The strained muscles of his shoulders and neck. The flare of his nostrils. The fact that his gaze had turned utterly unreadable.

Was he regretting this?

She should be shocked to be in this position. Yet it felt *right*. *They* felt right together.

Warmth welled in her chest, filling the place pain had hollowed.

Tentatively she smiled, clasping his face in her hands. The tickling caress of his beard felt better than velvet under her palms. She reached up to bestow a brief breathless kiss on his lips.

Tahir pulled back just far enough that she could see the light blaze in his eyes. His mouth turned up at one side, creating that sexy groove in his cheek she so adored.

The air smelt of the desert night, of the spicy musk of Tahir's skin, and of happiness.

Then he was kissing her, open-mouthed, slow yet passionate, as he moved within her. She gasped at the feel of his hard length sliding against her, igniting ripples of extraordinary pleasure.

He smiled against her mouth, his movements building to a steady pace that stole her breath all over again.

Then, abruptly, she began shaking. She was overloading on physical delight. Fire licked her belly, ecstasy sizzled along her nerve-ends and a quaking started deep inside.

'Tahir?' Her voice cracked as wave after wave of pleasure broke over her. She clung, suddenly scared.

His lazy smile was gone. But his look reassured her. 'Trust me, little one. Just let it happen. I promise you'll be safe.'

Not allowing her respite, he moved faster, harder, further, till she couldn't bear any more. Suddenly, gloriously, the volcanic force exploded into a starburst of euphoria. Wave after wave buoyed her up, till she floated high above the earth, suspended in utter bliss.

She heard his breath quicken, a groan as if of pain, then an exultant shout as he rocked faster, out of control, and suddenly the stars exploded again.

Through it all Annalisa held tight to the man in her arms, sensing for the first time a feeling of true belonging.

He felt like hell. Every bone and muscle ached. His head pounded sickeningly. He drew a slow breath and exhaled pain. The ribs he was pretty sure he'd bruised or cracked in the chopper crash hurt like the devil.

Yet he'd do it all again for the pleasure of seeing Annalisa experience orgasm for what he was pretty sure was the first time.

Heat ignited and his blood headed south at the memory of her gasping his name as she climaxed.

She'd been gorgeous. Glorious. Addictive. And the feel of her! The exquisite pleasure of being inside her!

He couldn't remember the last time sex had been that good. He doubted it ever had been.

Even though his memory had now returned, he could barely remember the last time he'd been with a woman. For months his libido had been non-existent. But he hadn't cared enough to worry about it. He'd given up caring about anything much these last years.

Too many years abusing his body with too little sleep, too many parties, too much alcohol, far too many women. Pushing the limits as he sought new challenges and pleasures. Anything to divert him from the grey pall that threatened whenever he stayed in one place too long.

Yet he'd been anything but bored in the dead heart of Qusay! With a woman who had no notion of how innately sexy she was. Who'd trusted and cared for him as no woman ever had.

An unfamiliar sensation slithered down his backbone. Regret? A pang of conscience?

It was so novel he concentrated his meagre energies on pinning it down. *Was* it conscience?

People thought Tahir Al'Ramiz didn't possess a conscience. He'd cultivated that view since he'd given up trying to be a perfect son and yielded to the weight of his father's hatred.

If you can't beat them join them.

Tahir had emulated his father in developing a taste for sybaritic decadence. By the time he was eighteen his family hadn't been able to stomach the sight of him. There'd been no tears shed at his exile.

But, despite his reputation for dissoluteness, he had some standards, even if he didn't broadcast them. He never harmed the innocent. He'd even privately helped a few of those who didn't have the benefits of wealth. Casual charity was easy. It didn't make him a good man. It was simple to give away what you didn't care about.

And he had never stooped to deflowering virgins.

Until last night.

That cold sensation was back again, slipping like ice down his spine and cramping his belly.

He didn't even have the excuse of amnesia. He'd known who he was last night: the sort of man who had no business consorting with innocents. He'd known his past, his present and, fate preserve him, his future.

Tahir hated thinking about the future. Other people dreamed of it. Like Annalisa. She'd been incandescent with delight about travelling and seeing the world. He'd been riveted by the sight of her excitement.

He couldn't remember ever feeling that happy.

His future would be the same as his past. Nothing significant enough to hold his attention.

Boredom.

Yet he hadn't been bored with Annalisa. The feral thought lodged in his brain.

Despite the pain and the infuriating slowness of his recovery, he'd enjoyed being here.

The realisation sideswiped him.

Talking with an inexperienced girl who'd never left Qusay about astronomy, the need for local schools, the latest plans for irrigating the edge of the desert. About customs he remembered from another life and people he'd never met, about the small communities that made up her world. Even about the care and feeding of an orphan goat. And he'd been content!

For days the bounds of this oasis had circumscribed his world and he hadn't hankered for more.

An image of Annalisa's smile appeared: the way her eyes softened when she laughed, the way the sun brought out gold and bronze highlights in her rich brown hair. The way her slim fingers felt as she tended his wounds. The scent of cinnamon and honey that haunted his sleep.

She was the reason he'd been content.

More than content. He'd been happy!

A sound interrupted his thoughts. Soft humming, off-key yet delightful.

He slitted open his eyes, seeing daylight. He'd slept late. He might even have been unconscious after the sheer stupidity of having sex despite cracked ribs and head wounds.

Ripping off his shirt last night had almost killed him. But he'd have died for sure if he hadn't felt Annalisa's hands on him, her sweet body against his.

His erection was instantaneous and achingly powerful, just at the memory of her.

The humming ceased and the tent flap lifted. His heart banged painfully against his ribs as she entered, wearing her hair down for the first time. Tendrils curled invitingly around her full breasts. She turned and a shaft of sunlight caught her back. Her hair rippled like finest silk, spun with threads of mahogany and gold.

She bent and retrieved something from the ground and his gaze fixed ravenously on the perfect peach shape of her bottom. His mouth dried.

Yet her movements weren't as graceful as usual. When she stepped across to tie up the tent flap he was sure of it.

She moved as if it hurt to walk.

As a woman might walk after a stranger had stolen her virginity. Then followed it up with a second bout of sex that had been far less restrained and even more desperate.

He'd been so needy. Despite his pain and her exhaustion he hadn't been able to resist kissing her awake and taking his fill of her again. He'd ensured she'd climaxed again, not once but twice. Yet he should have controlled himself. He should have known.

Hell! What did *he* know about virgins?

And, frankly, what did he care? Once he'd had Annalisa under him he hadn't been able to wait to have her again.

She turned and sunlight fell across her face.

What he saw there made his pulse thump out of kilter.

The cold feeling at his spine crept through his body, turning his organs to leaden lumps of ice.

Her once flawless skin was marred by angry reddened rashes. Around her mouth, on her cheeks and neck.

Whisker-burn.

More, there was a purpling mark on her throat. Another just visible at her neckline.

Where his teeth had grazed her.

Tahir's stomach swooped as it had the day his chopper crashed. But this time it didn't stop falling.

He shut his eyes against nausea as a vision from the past rose. His father staggering from a banquet with his closest, must corrupt cronies, his newest mistress tucked close beside him. Except his mistress had been a scared teenager who'd cringed at Yazan Al'Ramiz's touch.

His father had swatted him away like a fly when he'd tried to intervene, a skinny thirteen-year-old without the skill to tackle a full-grown man who knew every dirty trick. Tahir had gone down hard, cracking his head and coming to far too late to intervene again.

But he'd seen her the next day. Pale, with a livid bruise along her cheek. She hadn't seen him. She'd been too absorbed in misery to notice anyone.

The sound of Annalisa's off-key humming broke across the memory.

Last night hadn't been the same.

Annalisa had wanted him. Pleaded with him.

Except he'd used his sexual expertise to make her beg for something she didn't fully understand. He'd wanted her and set out to get her, even to the extent of having her admit it was *she* who wanted *him*.

As if that exonerated him.

Nothing changed the fact that he'd stolen her innocence.

Now she looked at him with stars in her eyes. Even through barely opened lids he saw her innocent wonder.

As if he was some fairytale hero.

As if he was the answer to a maiden's prayers.

The knot of glacial ice in his belly had sharp edges. It ripped his guts when he tried to breathe. It cut through his self-satisfaction and his excuses about last night.

It reminded him he was his father's son. Decadent. Self-interested. A man obsessed with pleasure.

The fact that Tahir found pleasure almost nowhere these days didn't alter the truth that he was as flawed as Yazan Al'Ramiz. He was the last man on earth she should be building castles in the air over.

For that was what she was doing. He could see it in her eyes. Annalisa was so refreshingly transparent.

Regret lanced him, so powerful it was a physical pain even stronger than what he already suffered.

He ignored it.

Annalisa would *not* be a casualty of his vices. She'd forget about him and get on with her life with never a backward glance.

He'd cure her of her romantic daydreams.

He owed her that much.

CHAPTER SIX

HE WAS awake. She caught a glimpse of his eyes, glinting like sunlight on the ocean. Her heart gave an awkward thump then settled into something like a steady beat, albeit far too rapid.

'I've made you breakfast.' She knelt beside him, eyes lowered, wishing she had the nerve to reach out and touch him as she had last night. But in the bright morning light she felt shy. It would be easier soon, when he smiled, caressed her. Maybe even tugged her down to him.

Heat sizzled in her stomach.

She wasn't sorry it had happened. Stunned, yes. Amazed at how beautiful it had been. But not regretful. It had been the single most wonderful experience of her life.

Tahir had been exquisitely tender and generous. She'd heard enough matrons gossiping about wedding nights to know not all women enjoyed their first time with a man.

Annalisa had done more than enjoy. Tahir had given her ecstasy. Warmth and connection and unbelievable pleasure. More, he'd bestowed something she couldn't name. Something glowing and positive that countered the pain of these last months. Something that made the future look sunny and wondrous.

'Not sweet tea again.' There was a petulance in his voice she'd never heard. 'Is that *all* you have?'

Her head jerked up and she met his frowning stare. His eyes were hard, almost febrile, his expression tight and unfamiliar.

The grooves around his mouth had deepened and his lips were pursed in a disgruntled line.

'Are you in pain?' What had she done, demanding so much last night? He was still far from recovered. Guilt slashed her and she reached out to him.

A sinewy forearm blocked her move. His eyes glittered and his nostrils pinched as if in displeasure.

'Of course I'm in pain. Having sex with these injuries was a fool's game.'

'I know. I've been wondering how you are.'

She waited for him to smile and say their night together had been worth the pain. That they'd shared something momentous and special.

The silence grew.

Tahir's gaze was unreadable. Something about his raised eyebrows and tight mouth made her sink back on her heels, her certainty suddenly on shaky foundations.

He *had* enjoyed it, hadn't he?

Of course he had. There'd been no mistaking his pleasure.

But maybe…maybe what had been a special, out of the world experience for her had been something else for him?

She clasped her hands, fighting the doubt roiling in her stomach. How she wished she understood.

Had he *nothing* to say about their night together? Even simply lying in his arms, tucked up against his large, powerful body had been bliss.

'I feel like you'd expect me to feel after a chopper crash, dehydration and over-exertion. I feel like death. Far worse than yesterday.'

Over-exertion? Annalisa frowned. That was what he called their lovemaking?

Over-exertion?

The churning in her stomach intensified even as a shaft of indignation hit her.

She tried to ignore it. Tahir was ill. By the look of him far worse than he'd been last night, and that was her fault. If she hadn't been so needy…

'I'll just…' She paused, his words sinking in. 'Chopper crash? You remember an accident?'

His mouth curved in a smile that held none of the rakish charm she'd grown used to. Instead he looked sarcastic.

'I wouldn't have said so if I hadn't remembered.'

'Were there others? On the helicopter?' The thought of people lost in the desert had haunted her for days.

'No. No one else to practise your precious nursing skills on.' The way he spoke made it sound as if she'd done more harm than good. Hurt and bewilderment curled inside her. Even as she heard his cutting words and saw his supercilious expression she didn't believe it. Tahir would never speak to her like that.

'But—'

'But nothing.' He paused. 'I had an important cargo, just not people. Crates of the finest champagne and the best caviar money can buy. I was bringing it here for the coronation, but I've missed the party now.' He lifted his shoulders in a stiff movement that confirmed his pain had worsened. 'A pity. If there's one thing I enjoy it's a good party.'

The way he said it, and his leer, implied something seedy and distasteful. No doubt he meant the kind of celebration no well brought up Qusani woman should know anything about.

She blinked, staring in disbelief at the changeling before her. Where was the stoic, witty, sociable man she'd cared for these past days? The one who'd been engaging and friendly, compassionate and even…loving?

He reached out an unsteady hand for the tea she'd brought. The way he clenched his jaw and the white line around his mouth told her his pain was extreme. Automatically she reached to help him, blaming herself for being so weak as to beg for sex from an injured man.

'Don't!' The single syllable was a harsh command. 'Don't touch me.'

Wide-eyed, Annalisa stared at the stranger before her.

Even in the extremity of his pain, even delirious, Tahir had never spoken to her in that tone of voice. As if she weren't worthy to breathe the same air as him.

Her heart squeezed in a spasm of acute distress. Pain, sharp as her grandfather's treasured sword, transfixed her.

'You've done enough.' His gaze slid from hers and he lifted the cup to his lips, grimacing in distaste. 'Let's hope they can at least make decent coffee in the palace.'

'In the palace?' Annalisa sank away from the mattress, lifting her knees and looping her arms around them, suddenly desperate for warmth, despite the hot shafts of sunlight illuminating this corner of the tent. She was cold on the inside. She felt as if she would never be warm again.

'Didn't I say I was heading to the palace?' He rolled his eyes as if in disgust at her ignorance. 'I'm a relative of the new king, Kareef. That's why I'm back in this god-forsaken country. To see him crowned, enjoy the celebration, then head back.'

'Back?' Annalisa felt absurdly like a parrot, repeating what he said. But her brain didn't work properly. She was still coming to terms with this shocking stranger.

It was as if, with the return of his memory, Tahir had undergone a personality transplant. From charming companion to the rear end of a camel in the blink of an eye.

The thought of her little cousin's favourite insult normally made her grin. Not this time. She tightened her grip on her legs, rocking slightly, as if seeking comfort.

There was no comfort to be found today.

If the pain lacerating her was any indication, she was bleeding internally—from the shattering of foolish, barely formed hopes.

How had she ever imagined she had anything in common with a man from another world? Who wore a tuxedo as if born to it? A man of obvious education and wealth and power?

A man, moreover, who had all the arrogance and none of the generosity that riches could breed.

She blinked hard, telling herself it was a speck of grit that made her eyes water.

'Back to civilisation,' he murmured. 'To the bright lights of the city. To business and sophisticated entertainment.' He lingered lovingly on the final words and bile rose in Annalisa's throat. She saw the glint in his eyes. There was no mistaking his meaning. Sophisticated *women*, he meant. With his looks and apparent wealth he'd have his fill.

The notion cramped her stomach.

What had she been? A passing whim? A novelty?

'No doubt you're eager to return to your friends,' she said, as brightly as she could. Unfortunately the words tumbled out rushed and uneven.

'You can't imagine how much.' He didn't even look at her, just picked at the carefully prepared food on the plate.

Annalisa's scalp prickled as nausea rose.

How had she been naïve enough to mistake last night for anything like tenderness or caring? She couldn't blame Tahir for taking what she'd offered—no, what she'd *begged* for so blatantly.

Shame suffused her, burning her cheeks and every place he'd touched last night.

But she couldn't forgive him for treating her with disdain. Did he think her lack of sophistication and experience a reason to view her with contempt? Was this her first taste of life in the big wide world?

Abruptly she raised her head, surprised to find him watching her.

She skewered him with a glare and lifted her chin, refusing to let him think she was humbled by his presence. Carefully she rose, ignoring the protest of aching muscles, then pinned on her best bright bedside smile.

'I'll leave you in peace. You'll want to make plans for your return to civilisation.'

When Annalisa's transport out of the desert arrived before noon, Tahir was ready to leave. He'd made himself thoroughly obnoxious all morning and could no longer stomach watching the effect on Annalisa.

At first she'd looked on in dazed bewilderment, her soft brown eyes brimming with disbelief. His conscience had smitten him like a hot branding iron across his already burning ribs.

Then, when she'd taken her measure of the 'new' Tahir, scorn and pride had made her lift her head and meet his jibes levelly. She'd looked regal and aloof and utterly lovely, confirming his belief that this was for the best.

But that hadn't stopped him craving her, like an addict needing just a little more. A smile, a touch, a caress. It had been hell, drawing her displeasure instead of her embraces with his arrogant nonsense.

Yet it was no more than he deserved.

He hadn't even thought of protection! Of pregnancy.

At the last moment, as the camel driver announced he was ready to go, Tahir cornered her. She'd decided to stay another few days. To study the skies, she'd said.

To lick her wounds, he was sure.

This was his last chance to talk to her.

'Annalisa.' Her head jerked up. She'd already said her goodbye, brief and stilted.

Her eyes widened and a flash of emotion warmed them for a moment. Her lips trembled open. In surprise or doubt?

Tahir clamped his hands behind him, battling the urge to reach for her. To soothe the hurt he'd inflicted. His voice when he found it was rougher than he'd intended.

'If there are consequences from last night...' His words petered out as the shocking image of Annalisa, blooming with good health and ripe with his child, blasted his mind.

'Impossible.' She shook her head. 'There won't be consequences.'

Tahir hadn't been born yesterday. If she tried to convince him she'd been taking contraceptives on the off-chance she'd let a stranger seduce her, she'd never succeed.

'If you're pregnant...' his voice dropped on the word '...I want you to tell me.' He held her defiant gaze so long that eventually she looked away. 'You can reach me via the palace.'

Silence. He cupped her chin, pulling her round to face him. The contact sizzled and he could almost swear he heard electricity crackle and spark as her eyes clashed with his.

How he wanted her! Even now, on the brink of farewell, his

body swayed forward and his hand tightened on her soft skin. Hunger gnawed at his belly, eclipsing even the burning pain that encircled his torso at every breath.

The temptation was almost too strong. Just one taste.

He dropped his hand as if burned. Took a step away.

'Promise me you'll let me know if—'

'So you can fund an abortion?' This time there was only scorn in her flashing eyes. She looked proud and dismissive as she eyed him up and down. 'There won't be any consequences. But if there were,' she hurried on before he could speak, 'I'd tell you.'

He nodded and turned away.

Minutes later he was seated on a camel. Its extreme motion, rocking perilously forwards then back as it rose to its feet, seemed expressly designed to torture a man with damaged ribs and a pounding head.

At least it took his mind off the contempt he'd seen in Annalisa's eyes.

The camels swayed out of the oasis, each step sending pain screaming through him. Even so, he mustered the willpower to turn and see Annalisa for the last time.

He needn't have bothered. She hadn't waited to watch him go. She'd already disappeared from view.

By the time they reached the coast Tahir was barely clinging on. Travelling through the heat of the day hadn't been sensible. If he'd been fit, perhaps, but with his injuries each kilometre was torture. The pain wrapping round his torso worsened and his head swam.

But he'd needed to get away while his determination held good. Before he did anything stupid like scooping her close and kissing her senseless.

He was surprised and grateful when his guide called a halt in a small fertile valley. They were still several hours from the capital, but Tahir could feel the last of his stamina draining away and he had no wish to slide off the camel in an ignominious heap.

It was only as they stopped in a pool of blessed shade that he realised the grove wasn't empty. A four-wheel drive and an ambulance were parked there.

He shot a questioning glance at his guide, already standing beside his mount.

For the first time his dour companion met his gaze directly, watching as Tahir's camel settled, lurching him sickeningly first one way then another.

'I called for assistance when we got within mobile phone range,' he said. 'Annalisa insisted.' His unblinking stare radiated disapproval. If he was a friend of Annalisa's he wouldn't have missed the undercurrents between her and Tahir.

Did he have a personal interest in Annalisa?

Tahir stiffened. His fists clenched and hot, scathing words hovered on his lips, ready to scare off this upstart.

Till he remembered he had no rights where she was concerned.

The realisation slammed into him so hard he reeled, and almost toppled over as nausea rose.

Finally, summoning the last of his strength, he lifted one leg over the saddle and slithered off. He stood, swaying drunkenly on ground that seemed to roll beneath him. His companion merely watched, arms folded.

'Your Highness?' A voice made Tahir turn, frowning.

'No. I—'

An older man, vaguely familiar, moved forward with a formal bow. For the life of him Tahir couldn't reciprocate. It was all he could do to stay upright on legs that shook mercilessly.

'Your Highness, let me express our heartfelt thanks that you've been delivered to us safely. We thought your helicopter went down over the coast and we've been searching the sea for days.'

At his nod two ambulance officers hurried forward with a stretcher.

Tahir opened his mouth to say he wasn't anyone's highness, then realised perhaps he was. With Kareef as king, that made him and their brother Rafiq princes.

The ludicrous notion of the black sheep of the family scoring a royal title pulled him up short. It was so outrageous, so bizarre, he barely noticed when his surroundings blurred around him.

He heard a shout, saw serious faces shift in and out of focus, then the world faded into oblivion.

He had to stop making a habit of passing out. He didn't have the patience for being sick. There was no amusement in it.

Even the soothing stroke of a soft, feminine hand at his brow lost its attraction when he came to enough to realise he'd dreamed it. What woman would sit patiently worrying at *his* bedside?

He'd had enough motor racing accidents to know nurses didn't caress their patients. And Annalisa, the only woman whose touch he desired, wasn't here. On the contrary, she'd be thanking her lucky stars she'd seen the last of him.

Still foggy from dreaming she was here, still weak enough to be plagued by regret that she wasn't, Tahir was in a sour mood when he woke.

He wasn't used to being dependent on anyone. Yet as he stirred he knew a craving for *her* by his side. He who'd never craved any woman! Who'd been alone so long he couldn't remember what it was like to wake up with the same woman twice.

He was in no mood to find himself hooked up to all sorts of machines. He was disengaging himself when the doctor arrived.

'No, sire. Please!'

Tahir ignored his protests. 'I don't need all this. I just need to get out of here.' Not that there was anywhere he wanted to go—unless it was an isolated oasis inhabited by the dark-eyed beauty he couldn't get out of his head.

The thought made him even more impatient.

There must be *somewhere* he should be. *Something* he should be doing. Something to keep him busy.

'I need to see my brother. I have business at the palace.' Tahir looked down in disgust at the hospital robe he wore. 'If you want to be useful, bring me clothes.'

'But, sire, you can't—'

Tahir waved aside his protests, ignoring the sharp stab of pain through his chest at the movement. 'Of course I can.'

'You don't understand, sire.' The doctor stood his ground and reluctantly Tahir focused on him. 'You need treatment and further observation. I can't take responsibility for releasing you yet.'

'I'll take responsibility. Just hurry up with those clothes.' Tahir forced himself to sit up and not sink back into the tempting comfort of the pillows. He felt absurdly weak.

'But, si—'

'And don't call me sire,' he snapped, ignoring the other man's hand-wringing. 'Just get me something to wear; that's all I ask.'

'Practising your fabled charm on the medical staff, little brother?' A deep drawl from the doorway drew Tahir's attention. He stiffened warily.

A tall man stood inside the door, his big frame suave in a hand-made Italian suit. His short black hair was brushed back severely and familiar ice-blue eyes surveyed Tahir.

After a moment Tahir saw the gleam of humour in his expression and the tension cramping his shoulders eased a fraction.

'Rafiq!' He hadn't seen his family in eleven years. Not since his father had banished him. The potent shot of delight that surged through him was a complete surprise.

He'd been so busy getting on with life, pursuing pleasure and business in equal measure, he hadn't let himself think about family. About resurrecting old ties. Even flying here he'd concentrated on the need to support his eldest brother, Kareef, as he ascended the throne, rather than on reviving personal relationships.

But the feel of Rafiq's solid hand gripping his, his other palm at Tahir's shoulder, as if to make sure he was actually there, evoked a blast of unexpected emotions.

'You're really here,' Rafiq said, his sombre expression transforming with a grin of real pleasure. 'Air control got your mayday, but there was interference and they misheard your coordinates and identification. They'd been searching the sea.' He shook his head. 'Why am I not surprised to hear you came out of the desert instead?'

Tahir felt an answering smile tug at his lips. He hadn't

allowed himself to think what sort of welcome the family would extend to the prodigal son, but he hadn't expected genuine warmth.

He returned Rafiq's grip with his own.

When he was a kid Rafiq and Kareef had been his role models. He'd striven to be as quick and as strong and as clever as they were. Particularly Rafiq, their father's favourite. But where Rafiq had been able to do little wrong in Yazan Al'Ramiz's eyes, Tahir had done nothing right. The unfairness of it had haunted him.

For a while Tahir had resented Rafiq bitterly, until he'd realised his brother had nothing to do with their father's favouritism. Or his frightening rages. In fact Rafiq had done his best to protect his little brother.

'You know I was always the contrary one,' Tahir murmured.

Rafiq shook his head. 'You were always a survivor. And I'm glad.' He nodded a dismissal to the hovering doctor, then pulled up a chair and sat, surveying Tahir with mingled amusement and consternation. 'You've been incredibly lucky, you know.'

'I know.' Even now, after days drinking all the fluids Annalisa had insisted on, he could taste the desert sand in his mouth. The flavour of death.

He'd been far luckier than he deserved.

Rafiq's grin faded. 'Do us all a favour, Tahir, and stay here. You need to recuperate.' He shook his head. 'You've got broken ribs and severe bruising, possible concussion, plus what the doctors warn is a severe chest infection. They say you're not in a good way. In fact they seem to think you're not as fit as you should be even without the injuries from the accident.'

Tahir shrugged. 'I've never cosseted myself.' And lately, as the darkness had closed around him more often and more swiftly, he'd pushed himself to the limits, seeking new thrills. He'd been careless of his health.

'Well, for pity's sake do it now. Just this once. Our mother has been frantic.'

Tahir's eyes widened. 'Our mother?'

Of all the people he'd left behind in Qusay she was the one

who'd weighed heavily on his conscience. Before his exile he'd tried to convince her to leave with him, lest Yazan Al'Ramiz turn his violence on her once he didn't have his scapegoat son to vent his anger on.

But she'd refused to see him, refused to take his calls. At first he'd thought it was fear of her husband that prompted her. But even after he'd left the country she'd wanted nothing to do with him. His calls and e-mails had gone unanswered. He'd assumed he'd alienated her too.

'You must be mistaken.'

Rafiq looked at him keenly. 'No mistake. She's been here since you were admitted, sitting by your bedside. She's only just left.'

Tahir remembered the comfort of a feminine hand soothing his brow and stroking his hand. He'd dreamed it was Annalisa.

Was it possible his mother, the woman who'd cut off all ties with him, was the one whose touch he'd felt?

It seemed preposterous. Yet Rafiq's concerned expression was real. Tahir frowned, trying to make sense of the impossible.

'I'm not imagining you, am I?' He'd suffered enough delirium in the last few days.

Rafiq huffed with laughter and settled more easily in his chair. 'Am I that ugly?'

Tahir's mouth pulled in a one-sided smile. 'You expect me to answer that?' He waved a hand in a gesture that encompassed the hospital room. 'This is just a bit much to absorb. And what's with these royal titles? "Sire" and "Your Highness" and so on?'

'Ah. I'm glad you mentioned that.' Rafiq leaned forward in his chair, his face suddenly serious. 'There's been a complication.'

'That's what Kareef said when he told me our cousin is no longer King of Qusay and that he would be taking the crown.' He watched Rafiq steeple his fingers and felt premonition spider its way down his spine. Something was wrong.

'Kareef has renounced the throne.'

'He's done what?'

'He and Jasmine… You remember Jasmine?'

Tahir nodded. His eldest brother had been besotted by her when he was eighteen.

'He's given up the throne to marry her and they've gone back to Qais to live.' At Tahir's stare he continued. 'Jasmine can't have children, and Kareef knows it's the King's duty to produce an heir.' He shrugged. 'You know how seriously he takes matters of duty.'

Tahir sank back against his pillows, absorbing this astonishing news. 'Looks like you've got a change of lifestyle ahead of you, big brother.' He'd seen a few articles about Rafiq's phenomenal business success in Australia. 'You'll have to move back here permanently. When do you take up the role of monarch?'

Rafiq paused before replying. He paused long enough to make Tahir frown again. That inkling of something wrong was back again, stronger than ever.

'That's one of the things I need to talk to you about.' There was no laughter lurking in his eyes now. 'I'm refusing the crown too, and moving back to Australia. Giving up the crown for love seems to be a family trait.'

'I don't believe it.' What sort of mess had he walked into?

'Believe it, Tahir. And as for the reason the doctor keeps calling you sire…? That would be because you're now King of Qusay.'

CHAPTER SEVEN

TIREDNESS took its toll and Annalisa's pace slowed as she walked along the wide esplanade in the capital, Shafar. She'd started out briskly from her aunt's house, needing to walk off her excess energy.

Her lips twisted ruefully. It wasn't excess energy but shock at the news she'd just received.

Yet part of her had expected it. Ever since she'd missed her period. Lately there'd been nausea, and a slight tingling in her breasts when she crossed her arms.

She'd thrust from her mind hints that her body was changing, telling herself it was the whirl of organising her overseas trip that had thrown her system out of balance.

What other cause could there be for her unaccustomed moping, her keen sense of distress?

A shudder marched down her spine at how wrong she'd been about Tahir. She'd known they were from separate worlds. Yet she'd believed herself...*connected* to him.

She told herself grief had made her turn to him for comfort. Wasn't she glad he'd shown his true colours? The return of his memory had revealed a man vastly different from the one she'd thought she'd known.

Demanding, dissatisfied, selfish.

She swallowed a knot of rising pain and stared dazedly towards the huge ornate gates set in the wall just ahead.

It didn't matter that their night together had been the most wonderful experience of her life. Was one night with an arrogant stranger, albeit a heart-stoppingly magical lover, worth the price she paid?

Her hand slipped across her flat stomach. It felt hollow because she'd been unable to face breakfast.

She'd imagined having children after marrying a man she loved. She mightn't be a traditional Qusani woman, but neither had she dreamed of being a single parent.

More than ever she felt the loss of her beloved parents and her grandfather. Her cousins were kind and caring, but they'd be shocked to the core by her news.

She shook her head, rocked by the emotions bombarding her. Excitement, fear, confusion and renewed grief.

Putting a hand to the wall beside her, she braced herself, fighting nausea as her stomach roiled.

It will be all right. Women have babies all the time.

Yet Annalisa felt bereft and shockingly alone.

'Are you all right, my dear?' The gentle voice made her turn her head.

A few metres away a silver limousine had stopped across the pavement, before turning into the massive open gates. In the back seat sat an older woman, with a severe yet chic hairstyle, gentle eyes and a fortune in pearls.

Hastily Annalisa straightened.

'Thank you,' she said, a flush scorching her throat. She felt exposed, as if she'd inadvertently displayed her private fears and worry. 'I'm fine.'

The woman regarded her carefully. 'If you'll forgive me, you don't look well. You're pale. Were you on your way to the palace? Did you have an appointment?'

Annalisa's head jerked round at her mention of the palace. She'd been so absorbed she'd barely noticed which way she'd walked. Now, through the ceremonial gates, she saw the royal enclosure's majestic gardens and the massive domed palace roof.

Her stomach tumbled over. Had she subconsciously come this way because of Tahir? What were the chances of him still being here? It was more than a month since…

Hastily she looked away.

If you're pregnant I want you to tell me. Promise me.

Tahir's voice was so real Annalisa shivered, her arms automatically wrapping around her torso.

'Are you here to see someone?'

'No!' The word shot out instantly. Then she paused.

She'd have to tell him. Even though she was almost certain he'd expect her to terminate the pregnancy. A father had a right to know he had a child. That much she knew.

And the fact that she wanted this baby, come what may.

The certainty warmed her, strengthening her weary body. Of course she wanted this child! She'd barely absorbed the news of her pregnancy, but that one fact tugged her lips wide in a smile of pure joy.

'That is…' She looked again at the woman in the car, so patiently awaiting her response. Was she a diplomat, or a friend of the royal family?

Tahir was connected to the King. Perhaps she knew him?

Annalisa took a few diffident steps forward, feeling gauche, yet impelled to follow this opportunity. 'I'm sorry, I'm a little…' What? Confused? Upset? Pregnant? She stifled a bubble of hysterical laughter.

'It's kind of you to ask,' she started again, pinning a polite smile on her face. 'I was hoping to contact someone at the palace. He's called Tahir. I don't know his family name. Tall, lean, bright blue eyes? He was injured in a helicopter crash.'

The woman's expression didn't alter and Annalisa's hope waned. It was foolish to expect he'd still be here. 'But it doesn't matter. He's probably not—'

'You met Tahir after his accident?' The woman's voice held a curious inflection.

'I… Yes. In the desert. I did what I could to nurse him, but—' Annalisa stiffened, alarm jolting through her at the woman's arrested expression. She moved up to the car, would have gripped the door if a burly guard hadn't stepped in front of her.

But she had to know.

She peered round him. 'He did get better, didn't he? He's

all right?' Tahir hadn't fully recovered. 'His head wounds—they weren't…?'

Fatal. She couldn't say the word, could only stare mutely and hope for reassurance.

For all Tahir had revealed an unpleasant side to his character, she *knew* there was more to him. He'd been kind, funny, likeable through those days at the oasis. And he'd been an exquisitely tender lover. The idea of him—

'No, no. Of course he's not dead.' A reassuring smile played on the other woman's lips. 'He's recovered now. According to the doctors, he owes his life to you.'

Annalisa's heart gave a great thump of relief and she lifted a hand to it, surprised at how shaky she felt.

The woman said something Annalisa didn't hear over the pounding in her blood. The guard moved, taking her elbow and ushering her to the far side of the vehicle. A chauffeur stood to attention, holding open the rear door.

The interior smelt of leather and expensive perfume. Annalisa's eyes widened as she took in the full impact of the elegant woman inside. She wore indigo silk exquisitely embroidered with silver. High-heeled silver sandals. Pearls at her wrist as well as her throat.

Annalisa froze, suddenly fully aware that this was someone very important indeed. The limo, the guard, her clothes, her air of understated refinement…

'Don't be shy,' she said, gesturing for Annalisa to enter the vehicle. 'You want to see Tahir, don't you?'

Mutely Annalisa nodded. She told herself she *needed* to see him. She had more sense than to *want* to see him. That madness had passed.

'Thank you,' she murmured. 'But if he's here I'll come back later, when I'm tidier.' She gestured to her clothes. Shoes dusty from hours of wandering. Loose trousers and her favourite green shirt: comfortable, but hardly appropriate for calling at the palace.

'Nonsense. Tahir will want to see you and thank you personally. I know he's here at the moment.' She beckoned, and this time Annalisa complied, gingerly settling herself on the wide seat.

The door clicked shut and she jumped, unable to stifle the

notion she'd committed herself to more than she'd intended. The car slid forward and Annalisa turned to her companion, wondering if it was too late to back out. She could talk to Tahir by phone.

'Your name, my dear?' The woman forestalled her.

'I'm Annalisa Hansen.'

'How do you do, Annalisa? I'm Rihana Al'Ramiz, Tahir's mother.'

Annalisa opened her mouth to reply, then snapped her jaw shut as she absorbed the name.

Al'Ramiz. It couldn't be...

Yet, taking in the other woman's attire, Annalisa realised with a sinking sensation it could very well be. Al'Ramiz was the name of Qusay's ruling family.

'How do you do?' Her voice emerged as a hoarse whisper. She paused, unsure how to proceed. 'Tahir said he was coming for a coronation.'

Rihana Al'Ramiz nodded, her mouth curving wryly. 'His brother, Kareef, has just inherited the throne.'

'But…' Annalisa shook her head, unable to take it in. Tahir was a member of the royal family! He'd said he was related to the King, but she'd thought he meant a distant connection. She was sharing a seat with the dowager Queen of Qusay! 'I had no idea…' she blurted out.

Her skin prickled and tightened and her vision blurred around the edges. Annalisa gripped the seat with shaking fingers as the world pitched and heaved out of focus. This was one shock too many.

'It's all right.' A gentle hand on hers tugged her back to reality. 'You'll feel better when you've had some refreshment. Come.' Her tone grew brisk as the door opened and a servant gestured for Annalisa to get out.

Shakily Annalisa stood, concentrating on staying upright. Her legs were like jelly and her bones felt hollow, as if a breeze might blow her away.

She watched Rihana Al'Ramiz gesture towards the beautiful old palace. Sunlight glinted off semi-precious gems set in decorative patterns around the entrance and servants stood to attention, waiting to usher them inside.

The sense of unreality grew. And with it the worrying suspicion that life was about to get even more complicated.

'Thank you for your advice, Akmal. The views of the Council are always of interest to me.' Tahir prowled to the huge window facing the sea and reminded himself for the hundredth time that patience was required.

Patience wasn't his style.

Ruling a country wasn't his style!

He couldn't believe after all these weeks he hadn't found a way out of this bind. Or that the Qusanis wanted *him*, the reprobate son of a vicious father, to succeed to the throne. But despite his best efforts he'd yet to uncover a distant relative who could take the royal role off his hands. As far as the Council of Elders was concerned he was King, and they expected him to rule.

He couldn't begrudge his brothers their decision to give up the throne. He'd do the same himself if he could. But he was trapped till he found a viable alternative.

'A suitable marriage would be timely, sire,' his vizier said in a measured tone. 'After the…turmoil of the last months it would be a perfect way of demonstrating the stability of the royal lineage.'

Tahir's mouth kicked up at one side. 'Turmoil' was Akmal's diplomatic way of saying the Al'Ramiz brothers had caused enough sensation for several lifetimes.

After his cousin Zafir had discovered he wasn't the legitimate ruler and stepped aside, Tahir's eldest brother had inherited. But as both Kareef and then Rafiq had since renounced the throne, the country now lay in Tahir's hands.

A man who'd been exiled at eighteen. The brother with the wildest reputation. Who hadn't set foot here for eleven years. He clenched his fists.

Hell! He couldn't stay as King. He wasn't into responsibility, or settling in one place long-term.

No wonder they wanted him to marry. They hoped it would make him settled and stable. *Tied down*.

'The Princess is—'

'Thank you, Akmal.' He spun around to face his advisor. 'I'm sure she's a paragon of virtue and would make a perfect queen.' He clasped his hands behind his back, remembering the old man was only doing his job in pressing for a wedding. 'However, it's too soon to consider marriage.'

'But, sire—'

Akmal broke off as a knock sounded and a servant entered, apologising. He was sorry to intrude, he knew the importance of the King's private meeting, but he—

'What is it?' Tahir was only too grateful for the interruption.

'The Lady Rihana asks if you would join her for tea, Highness.'

Tahir froze in mid-step.

His *mother* had invited him to tea?

It was unprecedented. Since he'd been back he'd seen her, of course. She'd expressed relief that he was safe. She'd welcomed him and offered her support. All with a distant courtesy that spoke of good breeding and duty.

Not a trace of maternal love.

He'd shattered that by the time he got kicked out of the country, after being found with his father's naked mistress.

It didn't matter that it had been the mistress trying to seduce *him*. Nor that Tahir had an ingrained distaste for the notion of sharing his father's women. But he hadn't protested his innocence. His father's fury had been worth the price.

Tahir had become a son no parent could be proud of. His mother's distance made it clear he'd long ago destroyed any vestige of parental devotion.

And now? Perhaps she needed something.

That was why people got close: for what he could provide. Money, sex, publicity, the excitement of walking on the wild side with a man whose reputation was notorious.

'I'd be delighted to join her.' Tahir turned to his vizier. 'If you'll excuse me?'

Akmal was already bowing. 'Of course, sire.'

* * *

He pulled up short in the doorway. Afternoon sunlight slanted through the deep-set windows. It caught golden highlights in a woman's rich brown hair.

His stomach clenched as memories stirred. Long silken tresses tangling round him as he shivered in pleasure and release. Smiling dark eyes looking shyly up at him. Lush red lips tentatively kissing his flesh. His heart had leapt at that gentle caress.

She turned and his heart ricocheted against his ribs, beating out of kilter.

'Annalisa!' He was halfway across the room before he remembered himself and took note of the situation.

Annalisa, the girl he'd left angry and hurt but well, looked far too pale. Her face was thinner, and her brow puckered as if she were in pain. Her lips were compressed in a nervous line and her eyes skittered from his.

He started forward again.

'Tahir. I'm glad you could join us.' His mother rose from a nearby divan and he slammed to a halt.

Swiftly he bowed. 'Mother.'

He sent her a searching stare, but she met his regard blandly. What was going on?

'Ms Hansen.'

Annalisa looked up, eyes wide with surprise. Last time they'd been together the circumstances hadn't been so formal.

Curling heat in his belly testified to just how *informal* they'd been. Blood pooled low in his body, a precursor to the heavy weight of arousal.

He stood straighter, stunned by his reaction. For months his sex drive had been absent. Till Annalisa. Since recuperating he'd felt not a twinge of interest in any of the local beauties. Yet one glance at her and…

Quickly he took the seat his mother indicated.

An antique tea service was laid out on a low table. A gold salver held syrupy cakes and figs. A laden plate sat before Annalisa, untouched.

'Ms Hansen has come to see you, Tahir. I met her at the

palace gates.' His mother regarded him steadily, her look now razor-sharp.

His skin tightened. What had Annalisa said?

'I knew you'd want to thank her for what she did in the desert.' She turned, smiling at her guest. 'We owe you an enormous debt of gratitude, Annalisa.'

Tahir accepted a glass in a filigree holder and murmured his thanks, his gaze straying to Annalisa's silent form.

Despite the Queen's hospitality, she was uncomfortable, her shoulders hunched defensively. He knew a burning need to reach out and gentle her, as he would a nervous filly. Instead he curled his fingers around his tea.

Where was the confident woman who'd nursed him? Who camped alone so self-sufficiently?

'How are you?' he asked, willing her to meet his gaze. She stared at a point near his left ear.

'I'm fine, thank you.'

The husky edge to her voice caught at his midriff, drawing muscles tight.

Something was wrong. He knew it with a gut-deep certainty even this stifling formality couldn't quell. He put the tea down with a click on the inlaid table. Had someone hurt her? The hairs rose on the back of his neck as unfamiliar waves of emotion washed through him.

The shrill ring of a phone intruded and Tahir got to his feet, eager for an excuse to move.

'It's for you, Mother,' he said moments later. 'Some crisis with the reception you're planning.'

His mother rose gracefully. 'If you'll excuse me, I'd better take this.' She paused, turning to Annalisa. 'If you'll be all right, my dear?'

Fiery colour flared in Annalisa's cheeks, yet her hands clenched so tight her knuckles shone white. 'Of course, ma'am. Thank you.'

Tahir waited till his mother took the phone into the next room. Then he turned, every sense on alert as foreboding chilled his blood.

* * *

She should never have come.

Afternoon sun highlighted the strong contours of Tahir's face, gifting his glossy hair with a luxurious blue-black sheen. His eyes were vivid and probing under straight brows.

He was more imposing than she remembered. She thought she'd imagined that potent allure, that heady male strength and the lazy sexuality of his smile. But one look, just the sound of her name on his lips, and she was in danger of falling for him all over again.

Even knowing how cold and callous he really was!

Had she lost her grip on reality as she struggled with one shock after another?

She stumbled to her feet when he approached and he stopped. Her heart pattered an unfamiliar rhythm.

'It's good to see you, Annalisa.'

She wished she could say the same. The traditional robe he wore emphasised his height and rangy power. He was too big, too confronting, too attractive.

Her breath expelled in a silent hiss as she realised her weakness for this man hadn't ended.

'Are you all right?' Her body came alive under his roving gaze. How did he do that?

'Yes,' she lied. 'I'm okay. And you?' The words were stilted but she had to know.

'Fighting fit.' His lopsided smile squeezed her heart and she looked away, frightened by the intensity of her feelings. She should be over him. He wasn't the man she'd first thought him. Besides, he came from a different world. He was royalty.

'I didn't expect to see you here.' He paced closer and she forced herself to stand her ground.

'I got to Shafar last night. I'm booked on a flight to Europe tomorrow.' But should she go? This morning's news changed everything. She bit her lip, wondering what to do for the best. A doctor's appointment was her first priority now.

'Something's wrong. What is it?'

His concern drew her gaze to his. If she didn't know better she'd think he cared.

She shut her eyes for a moment, willing herself to be strong. To snap the curious hold he had over her. When she opened them he was closer, a pace away. She swallowed at the illusion of warmth she read in his eyes.

Annalisa darted a look at the closed door the Queen had used. How long would they have in private?

'I needed to see you.' Only to herself did she admit she'd *wanted* to see him, craved it. She couldn't drag her eyes from him.

His brows tilted down. 'So this isn't a social call.' He paused. 'And it's obviously important. Not about the care of our stray goat?'

'It's gone to a good home. The youngest daughter of one of my cousins has made a pet of it.' Annalisa paused, aghast at her nervous babbling.

She shook her head, feeling her hair swirl from her ponytail, wishing she'd put it up so she looked more in control.

'You said…' She swallowed and made herself go on, lifting her chin to meet his gaze head-on. 'You said if there were…consequences I should let you know.' Something inside shattered as his expression remained cool and aloof.

'Well, there are consequences. I'm pregnant.'

Her words echoed in growing silence. His brilliant blue gaze grew laser-sharp but no warmer.

If she'd needed proof she meant nothing to him it was there in his shuttered expression and tightening jaw. The only sign of life was his throbbing pulse. Otherwise he might have been carved from stone.

She told herself it was what she'd expected.

Abruptly she turned, blinking at the view of a manicured courtyard bathed in the glow of afternoon sun.

'What are your plans?' His voice was harsh, grating her frayed nerves.

No talk of *our* plans or *his* involvement. What had she expected? For him to sweep her close and say he'd missed her? That leaving her was the biggest mistake of his life?

Bile rose in her throat as she realised some forlorn part of her had wanted just that. Had clung to the mirage of the man she'd fallen for before he'd shown his true self. As if it was possible to fall in love like that!

Annalisa shrugged, anger surging at her foolishness. 'I don't know. But I *am* having this baby.' Her hand inched protectively across her abdomen.

Silence.

Her lips twisted as she imagined his horror. He wouldn't want this complication. Unless he already had a trail of illegitimate children. The things he'd said that last morning made it possible.

She hunched as pain battered her.

'How convenient you found me here.' Something in his tone made her swing round. He looked more commanding than ever. Daunting.

'You told me to contact you.'

'And how could you pass up the opportunity when you found out who I was?' His lips thinned.

'Opportunity?' Annalisa groped for understanding.

He shrugged. 'To cash in on my position.'

For a full thirty seconds Annalisa stared into a face grown harsh with suspicion. Then his meaning registered and fire exploded in her bloodstream, rippling through every artery and vein.

She drew herself up straight.

'That doesn't deserve an answer.' Yet an outraged response bubbled up. 'You have some ego! A woman comes to tell you you've fathered a child and it's all about *you*?'

How gullible she was. Even after his treatment of her, she'd expected better.

'You deny my situation has anything to do with your claim to be pregnant?'

'Claim?' Annalisa remembered the days she'd fretted that pregnancy was possible. The fatigue and nausea. The panicked knowledge that she had to make decisions not just for herself now, but for her baby. Her hands clenched as she resisted a never before felt urge to slap someone.

'I'm pregnant. It has nothing to do with you being rich or the brother of the King. I only found that out when your mother told me.'

'And you couldn't resist sharing your juicy news with her, right?' His dark scowl was furious.

'I told her nothing!'

One eloquent eyebrow rose in disbelief and he crossed his arms over that broad chest, the epitome of male scorn.

Suddenly she felt dreadfully small and powerless.

'Then why was she so solicitous?' he pressed. 'Why leave us alone against every rule of protocol?'

Horrified, Annalisa widened her eyes. Had the Queen guessed? Her stomach lurched in dismay. Bad enough sharing the news with Tahir. She wasn't ready for the Queen's censure too.

'I was sick when we arrived. Morning sickness…'

'You didn't drop any coy hints?'

His words lashed her, his distrust stinging like the blast of a sandstorm on bare skin.

Annalisa wouldn't stay to be insulted. She'd done what she must.

But as she marched past he reached out and snagged her wrist. His touch was shocking heat against her flesh, making her pulse gallop.

'Let me go. Or am I supposed to make obeisance to such an important person first?' She'd never been one for sarcasm and her furious words surprised even her.

Tahir peered down into her face. 'Where will you go?'

'To my aunt's house. I have to pack for my flight.' She tried to tug free but his hold tightened implacably.

She breathed deep. 'Please, let me go.' His closeness confounded her outrage, weakening her fragile composure.

'You can stay here,' he said abruptly.

'No! There's no need.' She stepped back but he followed, crowding her. His scent invaded her nostrils and to her consternation she felt a flicker of response to its subtle allure.

'There's every need,' he assured her. The glint in his eyes

sent a shiver of doubt racing down her spine. 'We have things to discuss.'

Annalisa looked away. 'I won't stay where I'm not wanted.' He'd made it clear he thought she was inventing the story of her pregnancy.

'Oh, I wouldn't put it that way.' His voice dropped to a silky burr. His thumb stroked her sensitive inner wrist, brushing back and forth till her pulse raced unevenly.

Startled, she met eyes turned bright with desire.

Her breath caught in her throat as an answering tide of warmth spread out from her womb. One look from half-lidded eyes, one word in that bedroom voice and she melted!

'I'm going.'

Tahir shook his head, that flash of hunger doused as if it had never been. He looked grim.

'My family and I owe you hospitality for saving my life. Besides…' his long fingers tightened on her wrist '…I'll only have you brought back. Far easier if you stay.'

'Brought back?' Indignation warred with fury. 'Just who do you think you are?'

He inclined his head, sketching a graceful gesture with one hand.

'I'm Sheikh Tahir Al'Ramiz, King of Qusay.' His eyes flickered in grim amusement. 'I'm your sovereign lord.'

CHAPTER EIGHT

FOR the first time Tahir relished the fact he was King.

Because Annalisa couldn't escape till he was ready to let her go. He could demand her obedience.

Because he revelled in the power it gave him over this one woman. He felt a ripple of primitive pleasure any civilised man should abhor.

What did that say about him?

He scrubbed a hand over his face. Why couldn't the elders and citizens of Qusay understand they supported a flawed man as their monarch?

He remembered the dismay on Annalisa's face when she'd learned who he was. Busy in her outlying province, with her packing and her goodbyes, she'd heard Kareef had renounced the kingship, but not what had followed.

She hadn't known Tahir's identity.

The doubts that had swarmed on hearing her revelation had disintegrated in the face of her shock. Cynicism engendered by grasping lovers and false paternity suits had melted as he'd watched her struggle with the gravity of her situation.

Pregnant with the monarch's child.

No wonder she'd paled. She'd swayed, the dazed look in her velvet eyes evoking a protectiveness he'd known only once before. When he'd deliberately invited her scorn at the oasis so she could be free of him.

If only he still had such strength of mind.

He stared across the shadowed bedroom, past billowing curtains drawn aside to let in sweet night air. Moonlight covered the wide bed, gleamed on pale bare arms, caressed the dark fall of long hair across the pillow.

What sort of man was he?

One who couldn't master himself to keep away from a woman who despised him. Had he no shame? No scruples?

Yielding to temptation was a speciality of his.

Unable to sleep after hours working on official documents, he'd given in to restlessness and prowled the corridors. Only to find himself outside the suite set aside for the woman who was officially his mother's guest.

Here he was, a voyeur, rooted to the spot by the sight of her, fast asleep. She didn't wear silk or lace like his usual lovers. Just a white cotton nightshirt. Yet she looked utterly seductive and he was hard with wanting.

Tahir passed his hand over his face again. An honourable man wouldn't have entered her chamber.

He'd given up being honourable a lifetime ago.

His lips twisted in a savage grimace. What irony he should be named Tahir: 'pure'. He hadn't been pure in thought, word or deed since adolescence.

What business had he in this woman's chamber? A woman who was decent and trusting.

'Who is it?' Her voice was a thready whisper.

He stepped forward into silvery light.

'It's only me.' His mouth tightened derisively. That was meant to reassure her?

'What do you want?' She curled higher in the bed, drawing the sheet to her chin. Her defensive move amused and annoyed him. He hadn't yet stooped to attacking unwilling women.

'To see you.' It was simply the truth. But the need that had dragged him from the other side of the palace was neither simple nor straightforward.

In the dark he felt her regard, saw her lift her chin belligerently. 'You shouldn't be here.'

Once, the knowledge that he broke the rules would have

GET 2 BOOKS

We'd like to send you two *Harlequin Presents*® novels absolutely free. Accepting them puts you under no obligation to purchase any more books.

HOW TO GET YOUR
2 FREE BOOKS AND 2 FREE GIFTS

1. Return the reply card today, and we'll send you two *Harlequin Presents* novels, absolutely free! We'll even pay the postage!

2. Accepting free books places you under no obligation to buy anything, ever. Whatever you decide, the free books and gifts are yours to keep, free!

3. We hope that after receiving your free books you'll want to remain a subscriber, but the choice is yours—to continue or cancel, any time at all!

EXTRA BONUS

You'll also get two free mystery gifts! (worth about $10)

been an incitement, prompting him to outrageous action. But he'd barely given the proprieties a thought, simply yielded to his need to be with her.

'Your flight has been cancelled,' he said. 'The money will be refunded to your account.'

'You had no right to do that.' She sat up, propping a pillow behind her, and he caught sight of her lush, round breasts, outlined by fine cotton. His groin tightened.

'We need to discuss our options. We can't do that if you're in Scandinavia.' He should be grappling with the issue of her pregnancy, not this potent lust.

She folded her arms. 'You still had no authority.'

He stepped nearer, drawn by her sleep-husky voice. 'I've arranged for you to see an obstetrician.'

'I can organise that. You have no right to take over my life, forcing me to stay here.'

She sounded huffy. He was relieved to hear the spark of energy in her voice. She'd been so wan earlier. Was it normal for a pregnant woman to look worn to the bone? Or was it shock at discovering his identity that had sapped her strength?

'As far as the world is concerned, you are my mother's guest. What could be more pleasant?' He paused, acknowledging the need to keep Annalisa close was about his own desire as much as necessity. 'Now it's done, and you can reassure yourself everything's all right.'

'Or is it that you still don't believe I'm pregnant?'

He shook his head. When he'd heard her news he'd thought the worst, remembering the lengths women had gone to in order to snag his attention and his money. But within minutes he'd realised she wasn't bluffing. Annalisa was light-years from the sort of women with whom he usually consorted.

That was why the memory of their night together had burned indelibly into his consciousness. His gaze followed her lush curves under the pale sheet.

'I believe you, Annalisa.'

'Good.' Her voice was strained. 'Now you'd better go.'

'You wouldn't like me to stay and soothe you back to sleep?' One step took him to the bed. If he reached out…

'No!' Her voice held a telltale breathlessness that stirred the devil inside him, heating his blood.

'Perhaps I should persuade you.' He paused to drag in a surprisingly unsteady breath. 'I could, you know.'

He'd been taught by the best. Even his first sexual partner, the gorgeous girl he'd yearned for in his gullible teens, hadn't been the innocent he'd imagined. She'd enthusiastically shown him a myriad of ways to share pleasure before he'd discovered she'd bedded him not for affection but for his father's money.

And that he'd shared her with the old man.

The taint of that discovery had left him determined never to fall for anything approximating female innocence.

Until Annalisa.

'Is that why you're here? You want a change from your glamorous lovers?' Her voice dripped disdain.

She couldn't know how right she was. He yearned for her as he'd never yearned for any of the seductive beauties he'd bedded.

He couldn't recall feeling so *hungry* for a woman.

He stroked a finger along her bare arm, feeling her shiver in awareness. Instead of yanking her arm away she stilled. Tahir stiffened, iron-hard in arousal.

'How many have there been, Tahir? Dozens? Hundreds?'

'I'm no saint,' he growled, annoyed at her insistence on talking.

'I gathered that,' she murmured. 'I looked you up on the Internet this evening, since I had a name to search for.'

He froze at her frigid tone.

'Is it true you dated *all* the finalists in that Caribbean beauty pageant last year, in between closing a major business deal?' He watched her shift beneath the sheet and imagined his hands on her.

'The reports were exaggerated,' he murmured. A little.

'So is there a chance you've given me anything else, as well as a baby?'

For an instant he didn't follow her logic. Then his head reared back. 'You really are a doctor's daughter, aren't you?'

Annoyance warred with reluctant admiration at her temerity. No one spoke to him like that—ever. 'I may be reckless, Annalisa, but I'm not completely foolhardy. I have a clean bill of health.'

'I'm glad. For the sake of our child.'

Our child.

The reminder was a cold douche to his libido and he straightened away from the bed. He'd spent the last half-hour ignoring that complication. Far easier to focus on the delicious Annalisa than face the reality of a ready-made family.

Tahir didn't do family.

Couldn't do family.

He was a loner. Had been all his adult life. He had nothing to offer a child or a long-term partner.

He'd probably take after his unlamented father when it came to parenting. What if that defective gene had passed from the old man to him? Certainly he'd followed the old devil's footsteps in courting vice. Had his father seen that flaw in Tahir's personality from the first? Was that what had inspired such hatred of his own son?

The notion sent an icy shiver through his gut.

He'd never inflict his father's brand of paternal discipline on any child. Never risk that tainted strain appearing and harming an innocent.

He turned on his heel and strode for the door, his stomach churning. 'We'll talk later.'

'But not here,' she said quickly. 'I don't want you in my room. Ever.'

Tahir paused, the muscles across his back and shoulders tightening as if in response to a blow.

It was a sensation he hadn't felt for years. He couldn't remember it hurting this much.

'As you wish, Ms Hansen. I won't set foot in your room unless invited.'

Annalisa watched him go, her hand at her mouth to stop herself calling him back. She *didn't* want him here.

So why had she waited, quivering in anticipation, to see if he'd do more than stroke her arm? If he'd caress her properly?

Properly! There was no properly between them. She was pregnant with what would be his illegitimate child. She was a commoner and he a king.

He'd probably gone to meet some glamorous woman who'd be at home in the bed of a spoiled, aristocratic playboy.

What she'd read on the web had ripped the scales from her eyes. If a quarter of it was true Tahir was a man she couldn't begin to understand. A financial marvel, reckless gambler and lover of epic reputation. He strode through the ballrooms, boardrooms and bedrooms of at least three continents, taking what he wanted and moving on.

Stories about him were legion, but there was one common thread. He was a loner, never linked for long with any lover, not burdened with close friends or business partnerships. A man who needed no one.

And the man she'd met in the desert?

He hadn't been real. He'd been the product of Tahir's weakened state and extraordinary circumstances. He'd bedded her for the novelty of it. She couldn't be more different from the sexy women draped on his arm in the media reports.

The knowledge cramped her chest and she drew her knees up tight, curling into a ball.

Pregnancy was an enormous responsibility. Add to that the fact that she couldn't quash this craving for a man who saw her as an amusement and she was in deep trouble.

She'd even imagined something dark and troubled behind Tahir's careless demeanour. Had his nightmares in the desert been proof of that, or simply a fantasy brought on by delirium? She wanted to probe, uncover and confront the bleakness she sensed beneath his casual, sexy attitude.

She wanted to believe he cared.

Annalisa shook her head. She created excuses where there were none. She was out of her depth with Tahir.

In future she'd remember it.

* * *

'This way, please.' The footman bowed and Annalisa hesitated on the threshold of her suite. For days it had been a haven as she struggled to absorb the implications of her situation.

This period of peace and quiet had been what she'd needed. Sheikha Rihana, Tahir's mother, had been a daily visitor and, contrary to Annalisa's fears, she'd remained friendly rather than judgemental. The older woman must know of the obstetrician's visit yet she hadn't mentioned it. Did she guess at the fraught relationship between her guest and her son? That it was his child Annalisa carried?

They talked of everything but Tahir, and it felt as if a rapport had developed between them. Something more than good manners and hospitality. As if Rihana was as grateful for Annalisa's company as she was for Rihana's.

As for Tahir, after invading Annalisa's privacy that night, and hinting he'd seduce her, she'd expected to confront him the next morning.

Instead he'd left the capital on urgent business.

Only his personal intervention had saved regional diplomatic talks from foundering. Everyone sang his praises. But Annalisa suspected he'd found it a convenient reason not to face her.

Each day she braced herself to see him but he remained absent. *That told her all she needed to know about the importance of this baby to him. Her importance.*

'Madam?' The footman waited, his face expressionless. Did he wonder about her presence here? 'If you'll follow?'

Annalisa straightened her spine and stepped forward, following obediently down the wide arched corridor.

She couldn't hide for ever. Especially from her own kin. Yet when news had arrived that her uncle Saleem was here, her stomach had knotted. She'd never liked her aunt's husband. If there'd been an alternative to staying in his house when she'd arrived in Shafar she'd have taken it.

What did he want?

He'd never approved of her 'western' ways. Unlike the rest of the family, his relationship with her and her father had never been good. This couldn't be a social call.

Her tension increased as they progressed through the palace. Past sumptuous apartments and breathtakingly beautiful courtyards. Each inch was exquisite, from the inlaid floors to the luxurious furnishings and the view over a perfect indigo sea. They reached the public reception rooms where solemn visitors watched her with thinly veiled interest. Anxiety skated up her spine.

At every step she felt like an interloper in a world of privilege, prestige and protocol.

'Here you are, madam.' The servant opened gilded double doors. 'Refreshments have been provided. Please ring the bell if you need anything.' He stood back so she could enter, then shut the doors with quiet precision.

Saleem stood, feet wide, in the centre of the room. If he was awed by his surroundings he didn't show it. Instead he stood proud, a tall man, lantern-jawed and swarthy.

'Hello, Uncle. It's good of you to visit. My aunt hasn't come with you?' Annalisa kept her tone light, despite the chill that enveloped her as he scrutinised her like a beetle under a microscope.

'I came to see the King.' He paused on the word, investing it with distaste. 'I'm told he's not in, so I asked to see you instead.'

Annalisa stiffened at his bristling disapproval. This wasn't going to be good.

'Would you like a seat?' She gestured towards a group of elegant couches around a low table groaning with delicacies.

'You make yourself at home here, miss. As if you have every right to do so.'

'I'm a guest of the Sheikha Rihana. This is her hospitality and I—'

'Don't give me that! I wasn't born yesterday.'

He strode across to loom over her, eyes flashing.

Clasping her hands before her, Annalisa stood her ground. She'd seen him bully her aunt and refused to be cowed. Yet her pulse raced at how vulnerable she felt in face of his fury.

'You may put that story out for the gullible public but I know why you're here. You're *his* guest, aren't you? His mistress. His whore!'

Despite her resolve, Annalisa stumbled back, frightened by the violence in his snapping dark eyes and his bunched fists. Her heart thrashed against her ribs and the oxygen rushed from her lungs.

'I wonder he's got the gall to install you in the palace for all to see—but then, with his reputation, nothing should surprise me. A fine man you've chosen to give yourself to!'

Spittle flecked her cheek as he ranted and Annalisa cringed, the blood draining from her face. This was worse than anything she'd expected. Horror froze her to the spot.

'I'm nobody's whore,' she said breathlessly when she found her voice. 'You have no right—'

'I have *every* right. You're my responsibility now your father and grandfather are dead.'

Annalisa shook her head. 'No! I'm responsible for myself.'

'Not when you bring shame on the family.' His jaw thrust forward aggressively. 'I should have expected something like this, considering the freedoms you were given growing up. That father of yours—'

'Don't you *dare* say a word against my father.' It was Annalisa's turn to step forward and she saw surprise flash in Saleem's eyes. 'He was worth ten of you.'

For a moment there was silence. Blood pounded so hard in her ears she felt light-headed with the force of it. Distress, fear and fury were a sour mix on her tongue.

And guilt. Guilt at the way she'd fallen so easily for Tahir's facile charm.

'What would your precious father say if he could see you now?'

Annalisa swayed as if from a body-blow. Her father would be on her side. But how disappointed he'd be. He'd taught her the value of love. She'd fallen for its pale shadow.

'Don't you realise what you've done?' Saleem pressed on. 'The gossip about you and the King alone together in the desert for days?'

'What was I supposed to do? Ignore him when he stumbled into camp and leave him to die?' Annalisa planted her hands on her hips, finding relief in anger. She glared. 'If there's gossip, I don't have far to look for the source, do I?'

She guessed any such news hadn't come from the palace. The Queen didn't need to give reasons for inviting a guest to stay. Nor would it be from her other relatives, or the camel driver, who was an old friend of her father's.

Her suspicions were confirmed when Saleem spluttered, his gaze sliding from hers.

'You never liked me and you wanted an excuse to blacken my name.'

'Excuse?' he bellowed. 'What need for an excuse when you're pregnant? Ah, you didn't know I knew, did you?'

A sneer distorted his face and he grabbed her elbow in a merciless grip. Annalisa felt the walls close around her as shock and fear crowded close.

'You little slut. You were so caught up in your affair you didn't even have the sense to hide the evidence. Your aunt found the pregnancy test, clearing out your belongings when your lover sent his servants for them.'

Annalisa shrank from the hatred in his face.

'She was so upset I knew something was wrong. It didn't take much to get the truth out of her.'

Annalisa closed her eyes, praying fervently he hadn't used violence on her poor aunt.

A savage wrench of her arm made her flop like a rag doll. 'Now what have you got to say for yourself?'

'She'll say nothing to the likes of you.' The deep voice came from somewhere behind Annalisa, penetrating the haze of shock. 'Let her go. *Now*.' Tahir's voice dropped to a lethal rumble, like thunder on the horizon.

Instantly Saleem released her arm and she staggered a couple of steps away.

He'd heard the threat in Tahir's voice, for all the newcomer hadn't raised his voice. The air thickened, heavy with a menace more powerful than any of her uncle's taunts.

Swiftly she turned. Tahir stood feet wide, fists clenched. The sheer aggressive energy radiating from his tall frame was at odds with the urbane sophistication of his tailor-made suit. Never had she seen him so forbidding. His jaw was razor-sharp, his sensuous mouth firm. Tahir's face was austerely calm, but the light in his eyes was bloodthirsty. As if he wanted to tear her uncle limb from limb.

Relief swelled, buckling Annalisa's knees so she sagged against the back of a couch. She slid a shaking hand protectively across her abdomen.

'Your Majesty.' Her uncle bowed stiffly.

'Are you all right?' Tahir ignored him, turning to look at her. Even the concern in his tone didn't obliterate his distant, inflexible expression.

She wished he'd sweep her into his arms and hold her tight, till the trembling and the sick distress passed.

'I'm all right.' Annalisa was so shaken she didn't care that her voice wobbled with relief.

He swung round to her uncle, closing the space between them in a few strides. 'If I ever hear you've used violence on a woman, any woman, I'll make you wish you'd never been born.' The softly spoken words had the force of a cracking whip. 'And I'll know. I'll make it my business to know.'

'It wasn't violence, sire.' Saleem cowered back. 'It's a matter of honour.'

'You have a quaint understanding of honour.' Tahir's scorn was knife-edged. He turned his head again, looking over his shoulder at her. 'Can you walk?'

'Of course I can!' She stood up, away from the couch.

'Then go now. The footman outside will see you to your rooms.'

A cowardly part of her wanted to do as he said, escape from her uncle's ugly accusations. But she stood her ground. 'This is my business.'

For long seconds his deep blue gaze held hers, till tendrils of heat curled inside her, warming the chilled numbness. Finally he nodded.

'It is. Do you trust me to deal with it?'

Deal with Saleem? She had no doubts Tahir could do that more effectively than she.

Instinct overrode every doubt she had about his character.

He hadn't even acknowledged the baby was his, yet in this moment she knew no one could be a stronger champion for herself and her child.

'I trust you,' she murmured.

CHAPTER NINE

ANNALISA breathed deep of fresh, salty air, her hands twining restlessly. After that appalling scene she'd sought the garden overlooking the King's private beach. A quiet place to think.

But she hadn't been able to decide what to do. She'd been too caught up in reliving the horror of her uncle's accusations, and her overwhelming relief when Tahir had appeared. Just his presence had steadied her nerves.

Should she leave? Where would she go? To the village that had been her home? Could she expect the same treatment from the rest of her family?

Salty tears clogged her throat. Surely not. Surely they'd be more charitable. But right now she didn't want to test that.

She had to find a safe home, where her child would be welcomed, not scorned. She hugged her arms around herself, feeling more alone than ever.

Tahir had asked her to trust him, at least with Saleem. It confused her that she had. Shouldn't she be wary of the man who'd been shallow and callous? Yet now he'd stood up for her so forcefully.

'Annalisa?' A deep voice spoke as gravel crunched underfoot. She sat straighter and turned.

Her breath escaped in a sigh of appreciation as she devoured the sight of Tahir. Commanding nose, chiselled jaw and sapphire eyes that glittered under heavy lids. Sensation flared inside her. Desperately she told herself it was from gratitude that he'd dealt with Saleem.

Long legs ate up the distance separating them and she stood, feeling at a disadvantage sitting.

Besides, he was her king. She had to remember that.

'Thank you for dealing with…' she swept her arm wide '…with him. If you hadn't come—'

'Don't think about that.' He reached out, enclosing her hand in his. Heat engulfed her fingers and spread wondrously. 'It's over. He's gone.'

Was that satisfaction she heard in Tahir's voice? Surely he hadn't strong-armed Saleem into leaving?

'I'm sorry.' She shook her head miserably. 'You shouldn't have had to witness that.' Embarrassment fired her cheeks as she recalled all Saleem had said. Her skin crawled at his filthy outpouring of venom.

'Look at me!'

Tahir's abrupt tone jerked her head up. She met his bright, unblinking eyes. Somehow that steady regard strengthened her still-trembling body.

'You have nothing to apologise for. I'm just sorry I didn't arrive early enough to deal with him before you were called.' His lips curled in a tiny piratical smile. 'He won't bother you again. Ever.'

Annalisa didn't care how Tahir had done it; she simply basked in the knowledge.

'Thank you.' Profound relief coloured her voice and he inclined his head.

'How are you?' His grip tightened. 'Do you need a doctor?'

'Of course not.'

'You've been unwell.' His expression was sombre. Her pulse gave a shaky little jerk at his concern. 'The obstetrician was at pains to stress you need rest.'

She frowned. 'How do you know what she said?' At Tahir's bland expression futile anger spiked. 'So doctor-patient confidentiality doesn't apply at the palace?' She pulled her hand free and paced, restless at the discovery her privacy had been overridden.

Annalisa had never felt more powerless than in these last days, when her life had been turned upside down.

She was used to making decisions, being useful and active. Now she was in limbo, unsettled and unsure of herself. She'd thought today's interview with Saleem the final straw. Now she discovered she didn't even have exclusive rights to information about her own body.

She felt caged, no longer in control of her life.

'I was concerned for you.'

'Really?' She met his eyes. Fervently she wished she couldn't remember how they'd glowed with approval as she'd climaxed beneath him. Such memories underscored a weakness she couldn't conquer.

'It was unpardonable to leave you at such a time. I'm sorry.'

Her surge of indignation deflated abruptly with his apology. He was the monarch. He had other responsibilities.

'You were needed elsewhere. I understand.' Suddenly she felt exhausted.

'That's no excuse. My presence at the negotiations was more or less symbolic.'

Why did he brush off his vital part in the treaty talks? She frowned. Surely a shallow man who revelled in his prestige would brag about his pivotal role?

'You should rest.' A hand at her elbow propelled her to the seat and she subsided, Tahir beside her. His body warmed her even where they didn't touch.

It felt as if he drew her close with an unseen force field. Annalisa breathed deep and told herself she imagined the zap and crackle of electricity between them.

'It's time we resolved this,' he said finally.

'What?' she said wearily. 'You want a DNA test to prove the baby is yours?'

His fingers flexed and his hand dropped away.

'I know it's mine.'

Annalisa swung to meet his gaze head-on, plunging into clear depths that glinted with an expression she couldn't name.

'You've changed your tune.' It didn't matter that an hour ago he'd championed her against Saleem. It still rankled that Tahir had doubted her word.

His nostrils flared and he straightened, as if unaccustomed to being challenged. 'The news came as a shock.'

'You thought I was lying.'

'It wasn't the first time a woman had said she carried my child.' His gaze bored into hers. 'But it's the first time it was true.'

Bile rose in Annalisa's mouth. She was simply one in a long line of women. A notch in his belt. Only she hadn't been sophisticated enough to prevent her pregnancy.

'So you believe me now?'

'I believe you. I know you.'

Fervently Annalisa wished she could say the same. Tahir confused her. Was he a careless, selfish hedonist, or a man of sense and compassion? He altered each time she saw him. No wonder she felt disorientated.

'Unfortunately your uncle's visit changes things. There's no chance now of keeping our relationship private.'

Relationship? It was on the tip of her tongue to say they *had* no relationship. Just a one-night stand.

'What do you suppose he'll do?' She felt sick, thinking of the vitriol he'd pour into waiting ears.

'Nothing. He won't say a word to anyone.'

Annalisa opened her mouth to protest that Saleem would surely continue gossiping. Then she saw Tahir's expression and a chill pierced her. She wouldn't like to be in Saleem's shoes.

'But he's already said enough. When your pregnancy starts to show people will remember his words and put two and two together.'

Stupid, but she couldn't prevent a fillip of pleasure that Tahir had accepted she'd have the baby. That he hadn't tried to push for a termination.

'They'll know the baby is mine.'

'If I'm in Qusay.' Yet she couldn't imagine raising her child anywhere else.

'It doesn't matter.' His voice was terse. 'The damage is done. Wherever you are this will catch up with you. There's no escaping.'

His words carried the weight of a judge delivering sentence. The hairs on her nape stood up at his bleak tone.

'There's only one option.' He drew in a slow breath, as if delaying the pronouncement. 'We must marry.'

The words echoed in her disbelieving ears.

'You've got to be kidding!'

'You think I'd joke about this?' He shot to his feet to pace before her. 'You think I *desire* marriage? That I haven't considered every alternative?'

Annalisa read disdain in the proud lines of his face. A bone-deep distaste that shrivelled something in the pit of her stomach.

What he meant was he had no desire to marry *her*.

The fact that she wasn't ready for marriage either didn't ease the pain of his rejection.

Tahir's eyes were glacier-cool and her heart plunged. Did he think she'd tricked him into this? What other reason for that terrible distant look?

'I didn't know Saleem would come here. I didn't intend for anyone to know.'

He swatted aside her protestations with a slicing gesture. 'I know. That's immaterial. What matters is our solution to the problem.'

He didn't sound like a man proposing marriage.

She pressed shaking hands together, painful memories resurfacing. Dreams she'd spun years ago when she'd begun to fall in love with Toby.

Annalisa had expected a marriage proposal then.

It had never eventuated. Toby had gone back to Canada, taking up a new job as a geologist. Instead of returning for her, as promised, news had arrived months later that he'd married someone else. Someone 'from home'. Who fitted his world, his expectations.

Not someone like Annalisa, who straddled two cultures and was viewed as alien to both.

Was she doomed always to be an outsider, unworthy of love?

'Marriage isn't the only solution.'

When she married it would be for love. Like that her parents had shared. Her father had loved his wife till the end. His whole focus those last days had been surviving long enough to name the Asiya Comet for her.

A cold-hearted marriage to a cold-hearted man would be disaster. Even with her inexperience Annalisa knew that.

'What else is there? For you to bring up my illegitimate child under my nose?'

She raised her chin. 'Would it be the first?'

'I've already told you.' Tahir bit out the words with a re-strained savagery that made her shrink back. 'No other woman has carried my child.'

Spoken like a man with a soft spot for the woman he planned to marry!

'It needn't be under your nose.'

'You intend to emigrate?'

Silently she shook her head, feeling harried. This was too much, too soon. What should she do for the best?

'You *want* our child born illegitimate?'

'No,' she said miserably. 'But I don't want…'

'What don't you want, Annalisa?'

She bit her lip, not daring to voice the fears crowding close. How could she tie herself to a man she barely knew? A man she'd naïvely believed she…cared for, only to discover she didn't know him at all.

Could she trust a man of his reputation? Give herself and her baby into his keeping? In Qusay a husband had real power over his wife. His word was law.

If that husband was also King… They were poles apart, sep-arated by an unbreachable gulf.

'Annalisa, look at me. Talk to me.'

Slowly she turned. He leaned close, broad shoulders block-ing the view. His powerful presence pinioned her as if he held her in his arms.

If only he *would* hold her. Sweep her into his embrace as he had in the desert. She wanted to lean in and let him comfort her, care for her. But allowing herself to trust him in such a way would pose a dangerous threat to her already vulnerable heart.

She looked up into eyes bright as gems, at a mouth firm and decisive, a chin that jutted just a little aggressively as he waited for her to speak.

'Thank you for the offer,' she said in a low voice. 'No...' She looked away. 'I don't know. I need time.'

She needed time!

How much time did she think there was before her pregnancy became obvious? Before she became the subject of cruel jibes? Before she was shunned for her liaison with him?

Did she want that for herself and her baby?

Guilt punched hard in his gut. This was his fault. He'd given in to temptation and she'd pay the price.

Annalisa was so proud, so obstinate, and she wouldn't let him help her. Couldn't see how much worse the scandal would be because of who he was and what he'd been. The memory of that scene with her uncle curdled his stomach. He couldn't let her face such prejudice alone.

Or his child. Tahir had experience of being hated as a boy. He refused to give anyone the chance to hold *his* child in contempt.

He raked a hand through his hair as he paced his vast apartments, a sullen mix of emotions boiling over as he recalled her hesitation.

Since when had any woman said no to him? Women fell like ripe peaches into his open palm. Yet *this* woman hesitated. This little mouse, unsophisticated and innocent.

At least she had been till Tahir met her.

He had to make this right. Even if she didn't want him to. Even if she didn't want *him*.

The absurdity was that, with beautiful women put forward daily for his approval by those hoping he'd marry, it was Annalisa he wanted.

He felt a stirring in his groin and pounded his fist against the wall. It didn't matter what he *wanted*.

This was about necessity.

The thought of becoming a husband and father made him break out in a cold sweat. As usual, his desires were less honourable. It was sexual gratification he dreamt of, night after night. He hungered for Annalisa as he hadn't hungered for any woman.

Yet he couldn't leave her to cope with pregnancy and child-rearing alone. Not with *his* child. He might have lived the life of a reprobate, but he wasn't a complete moral vacuum.

Qusani society wasn't designed for unmarried mothers. The scene with her uncle had reinforced that. She'd never fit in and nor would the child—especially when it became known that Tahir was the father. They needed protection, even if the idea of acquiring responsibility for a family left a chilled lump in the pit of his belly.

He remembered his father, presenting an acceptable face to the public. Yet in private he'd been a cruel brute. Such a man shouldn't have children.

What if Tahir shared that same taint?

He didn't have his father's taste for violence. He didn't get kicks from bullying those weaker than himself. Yet, with his family history, who knew what sort of husband and father he'd make?

Rafiq and Kareef were brave men, embarking on married life with enthusiasm. But the taints of character had been Tahir's, not theirs. Their father's rage had always been directed at him, not his brothers.

When Tahir had recently visited his brother, in his new kingdom of Qais, Kareef and Jasmine had been ecstatically happy. Marriage suited Kareef. But he and Tahir were poles apart.

Tahir's lips flattened derisively at the notion of himself protecting Annalisa. Yet it had to be done.

He was tempted simply to organise the wedding despite her protests. He wasn't used to waiting. Yet he'd seen how shaken she was. She really did need time. He'd make one more attempt to make her see reason.

Heat kindled in his belly and he smiled at the thought of *persuading* her.

CHAPTER TEN

THE royal reception ran smoothly: the hum of conversation was steady, guests were smiling as they enjoyed the honour of being in the gilded audience rooms.

Tahir nodded to an ambassador.

Strange how easily he fitted this role. He worked long hours. But his talents for turning a deal, weighing situations and acting decisively were assets that made his royal role easier.

Except with Annalisa.

She'd managed to avoid him for days. Frustration gnawed at his belly.

He wanted this settled. Not because he wanted Annalisa, he assured himself, ignoring the nightly erotic dreams that kept him sleepless.

He stared past a cluster of businessmen and found her instantly. He'd been attuned to her presence since she'd entered the reception with his mother.

One look at Annalisa in shimmering amber silk and he couldn't concentrate on anything else. He imagined he heard her soft laughter over the noise of the exquisitely dressed throng.

She was smiling.

The sort of smile she hadn't given him since their night together. The sight punched a hole through his gut.

She smiled at a man: young and good-looking.

Tahir stiffened.

She tilted her head, as if to hear what her companion said. The man moved closer, cutting her off from the crowd.

Like a man with a woman he wanted, separating her so she could concentrate on him. Tahir knew the manoeuvre, the subtle shift of posture, the intimate tone, the extended arm gesture that made it seem they were alone.

He'd used that tactic himself, countless times.

Fury vibrated along every nerve. A proprietorial anger that demanded instant action.

'Pardon me.' He bowed to his companions with rigid decorum. 'I'll look forward to exploring this project in more detail with you. My staff will arrange a meeting.'

His companions murmured their thanks, and then he was striding across the room, deliberately not meeting the looks of those trying to catch his eye.

His attention was riveted on the woman in amber. Her gown was demure, yet the tracery of gold embroidery at its neckline drew the eye to the sweet swell of her breasts. When she moved the fine silk slithered over luscious curves that made his mouth water.

His fingers curled possessively.

She was his. No matter how she denied it.

The knowledge beat a primitive tattoo in his blood.

For hours he'd done his duty. It was time to act as a man, not a king.

'Really? That's fascinating,' Annalisa murmured, surreptitiously shifting back half a pace.

She'd enjoyed this conversation until her companion had closed the distance between them and the atmosphere had suddenly become intimate. Had she unwittingly encouraged him to think she was interested in him, not in his plans for dry land farming?

Annalisa was so used to sharing her father's discussions with visiting experts she'd responded openly and enthusiastically when Rihana had introduced them.

She should have followed her instinct and stayed away

tonight, despite Rihana's persuasion. Circumstances were different now. She didn't have the freedom of her father's protection to chat with strangers like an equal.

The scene with Saleem had reinforced that. She had to fit Qusani expectations. *Something she'd never been able to do*.

Distress and regret stifled her. She turned her head, seeking Rihana's reassuring presence. Instead she discovered searing blue eyes staring at her from under disapproving dark brows.

Annalisa caught her breath on a gasp and her companion swivelled, stammering, 'Your—your Majesty.'

Tahir inclined his head briefly. 'I'm not interrupting?'

The look in his eyes said he didn't give a damn if he was.

'Of course not, sire,' the young man replied hurriedly. He looked from Annalisa to the Sheikh looming beside them, then scuttled away, murmuring excuses.

At Tahir's blatantly disapproving look Annalisa felt a surge of anger rise. She hadn't done anything wrong.

Demurely she bowed her head. 'Your Highness.' She let her tone tell him what she thought of his attitude.

For one heady moment she'd thought he'd searched her out because he wanted her company. How pathetic could she be? The reception included plenty of sophisticated, beautiful women and Tahir had talked with all of them.

'Don't *Highness* me, Annalisa. It's too late for that.'

The acid in his voice jerked her head up. Thank goodness he was speaking so softly no one else could hear.

'And don't look for anyone else to rescue you.' He bit the words out through gritted teeth. 'No one will interrupt.' His mouth twisted wryly. 'That's one of the perks of being King.'

'I wasn't looking for rescue.' She tried to still her galloping pulse and slow her breathing. Her weakness for him horrified her. 'Why would I need rescuing?'

'If you flirted with me the way you did with him, I'd be tempted to flirt back. And, believe me, I wouldn't be as easy to shake off.' His lips drew wide in a feral smile.

Something fluttered deep inside her. Excitement.

'I wasn't flirting.' Annalisa lifted her chin, but she couldn't prevent a guilty flush staining her face. It wasn't her fault her companion had misunderstood. Was it?

One step brought Tahir close. His warmth enveloped her. If she moved a fraction they'd be touching.

Around them she heard a ripple of speculation sharpen voices, then an expectant lull as conversation ebbed.

Her heart thudded against her ribs and she felt again that curious tightening in her womb. Her body recalled too well the delights they'd shared, no matter how she tried to forget.

She sucked in a deep breath, then wished she hadn't as the movement brought her breasts close to his torso. Heat zapped between them and the air crackled.

Annalisa stepped back, pulse skittering.

He followed, closer than ever.

'Don't,' she whispered.

'Why not?' One eyebrow arched.

'Everyone is looking.' She felt the stares, heard the whispered speculation.

'So?' His mouth twisted in a cruel smile. 'Shouldn't you get used to it? If you're going to bear my bastard you'll always be the focus of gossip.'

Annalisa gasped, her body stiffening as if under a blow. She shuffled back another step, hand spread over her juddering heart. How could he be so…merciless? There was no sympathy in that proud, powerful face. Just disdain and a shadow of anger.

'Don't speak of it that way,' she whispered.

'Can't face the truth, Annalisa?'

Pain sheared through her. It *would* be the truth. Because she'd been foolish enough to give herself to him. Because, despite the threat of scandal, she was scared to marry Tahir. Such a union would stifle her. She and her baby needed love. Could they get that from a convenient marriage?

'This isn't the place to discuss it.' She dredged up her battered self-respect and met him stare for stare.

'Then we'll go elsewhere.' He paused. 'I warn you, if you're thinking of staying to snare another man it won't work. I'll make sure of it.'

Outrage doused her pain. 'Don't be absurd,' she hissed. 'You're mistaking me for someone else. I have no interest in *snaring* any man.'

'Not even to find a gullible, alternative father for—?'

'Not even for that!'

How could he *think* it? Had he *no* notion how momentous their short relationship had been for her? Did he really think she'd scheme to marry another man?

That she'd give herself so easily to another?

Annalisa's anger grew white-hot, and with it a hurt that stabbed her to the core. Tears burned her eyes and she turned to stare, blinking, across the room as if absorbed in the colourful scene. The depth of her pain appalled her.

'I wasn't flirting.' She drew a shuddering breath. 'I was just…talking. He was interesting, okay? And I've missed…'

'What have you missed, Annalisa?' His voice had lost its accusatory edge. It sounded almost regretful.

She shook her head. Tahir wouldn't understand. The man she'd shared so much with in the desert was no more. She couldn't bring him back, no matter how she wished it.

'Annalisa.' He moved close, stepping into her line of sight. 'I'm—'

'There you are, my dears.' At the sound of Rihana's voice Annalisa blinked furiously and pasted on a shaky smile. She turned to find her hostess bearing down upon them. The dowager Queen smiled, but the smile didn't reach her eyes.

Annalisa's heart sank. Did Rihana think she'd caused the disturbance?

'You mustn't monopolise our guest,' she scolded.

To Annalisa's surprise the older woman slipped her hand through Annalisa's arm and turned to face Tahir. A look passed between mother and son that she couldn't decipher, but she felt tension hum in the air.

'Especially,' Rihana continued, 'when you're the centre of attention. Whatever you have to say can be said in private. Our family has already provided enough gossip.' Her smile belied the steel in her tone.

Astonished, Annalisa realised the Queen was warning her son off. She was protecting Annalisa from Tahir.

Annalisa felt a surge of gratitude. How would she react when she realised the true situation between Annalisa and Tahir? Annalisa dreaded to think.

'As always, Mother, you're right.' Tahir sketched an elegant bow, then turned to Annalisa. 'As you said, this is neither the time nor the place.' He paused. 'We'll finish our conversation later.'

With a smile that would have fooled most people into believing he was in high good humour, Tahir left them.

Annalisa exhaled shakily, torn between relief and regret that they parted on such terms.

Rihana patted her hand. 'I hope you can forgive Tahir. He hasn't yet learned patience. He's been getting his own way for too long.' She turned, and Annalisa was struck by the sadness in her eyes. 'But it wasn't always that way. And the shame of it is he never got the one thing he wanted above all. The one thing that really counted. All the rest meant nothing.'

What was it? That one thing Tahir wanted most? Annalisa needed to know—to understand the man who stirred such strong, conflicting emotions in her.

For a moment she thought she saw a glimmer of tears in the other woman's eyes. But it must have been an illusion, for now Rihana was perfectly poised. She patted Annalisa's hand again.

'If you give him time I know you'll find him…' she paused '…worth the effort.'

When Annalisa went to her room later a tall shadow detached itself from an alcove near her door.

Though she'd expected him, her pulse jittered nervously as she followed Tahir. His silence in the empty passageways and the set of his broad shoulders increased her awareness of him as a man, powerful and potentially dangerous.

They emerged into the garden where he'd announced they'd marry. Had he chosen it deliberately? She twisted her hands together, her nerves close to shredding. Moonlight on the bay gave the scene a romantic feel. Or would have if she didn't recall Tahir's words stripping her to the bone.

She ignored his invitation to sit.

Silvery light threw one side of his face into shadow, emphasising the strong lines and aristocratic planes of his face. And the grim set of his mouth.

Annalisa stood straight, ready to counter more accusations.

'Your mother thought I'd enjoy meeting your guests tonight, and I did.' She refused to apologise. It wasn't she who'd created a scene.

'As for the gown…' She plucked nervously at the exquisite outfit she'd adored from the moment Rihana had produced it. 'Your mother kindly provided it because I didn't have anything suitable. Of course I won't keep it.' She refused to be accused of mercenary ways.

'My mother has taken a shine to you.' His voice revealed nothing.

Annalisa shrugged. 'She's lovely. And so lively, so interesting.' She watched one sleek black eyebrow climb. Did he doubt her sincerity?

'She's been very kind to me.' It emerged as a challenge.

'I can see that.' He surveyed her from head to toe and heat sizzled through her at his leisurely inspection. He had the lazy air of a pasha inspecting a new slave.

She stiffened, crossing her arms.

'There's no need to justify yourself,' he murmured. 'Of course you'll keep the dress.' He raised a silencing hand when she opened her mouth to protest. 'And you were welcome at the reception.'

His mouth quirked in a shadow of the lopsided smile she knew so well and her stomach gave a disturbing little jiggle. 'I've had two diplomats, the Chair of the Literacy Commission and countless others remarking how they enjoyed your company.'

'Really?'

Then what was his problem? She hadn't pushed herself forward, trying to embarrass him. Why had he been angry?

'Really.' Tahir lifted a hand, then paused, before spearing

his dark locks in a gesture of frustration. Abruptly he turned and paced away, then back again.

'I'm sorry for my behaviour tonight,' he said finally, his voice a low rumble. 'It was inexcusable, especially in public. I saw you with him and I…' Tahir made a slashing, violent gesture.

Clearly he wasn't used to apologising. But Annalisa sensed there was more. She stared. If it weren't so preposterous she'd think Tahir was *jealous*.

Impossible! To be jealous Tahir would need to care. He didn't.

'You don't accept my apology?'

Surprised, she noticed his indignant expression. Clearly humbling himself was a new experience.

'No, I— That is, yes. Of course.'

'Good.' He met her eyes with a seriousness that reminded her of the man she'd known at the oasis.

The man she'd fallen for.

Annalisa drew a sustaining breath and told herself to stop fantasising. But she couldn't prevent the spark of warmth that look had engendered. She'd felt it when he'd protected her from Saleem too.

'You've had days to think, Annalisa. Days since I said I'd marry you. I've been more than patient.'

Her pulse thrummed a heavy beat, quickening as she met his gaze. He reached out and clasped her hand, raising it between them. He held her lightly, yet instantly longing swamped her. Indignation and hurt were forgotten.

'It's not what either of us wants. But we're trapped by circumstance.' His voice deepened. 'You know in that logical head of yours this is the only way.'

Before she could respond he lifted his other hand and brushed a strand of hair behind her ear. Her breathing faltered and her cheek tingled where his knuckles brushed.

Yearning rose, swift and undeniable. She shouldn't respond. Yet her eyelids flickered, weighted under the impact of the glint in his eye.

There were times, like now, when she longed to trust Tahir.

Forget her doubts and fears and accept his strength. Times when her dreams sank beneath the weight of what she felt for him. Because she was off-balance in this harsh new reality? Because she felt so alone and bereft of friends?

Tahir's fingertips brushed her cheek again, swept to her chin and then her throat. Annalisa swallowed hard, remembering the sweet ecstasy he'd wrought with his touch once before.

She wanted Tahir so badly.

Feather-light, his fingers trailed to her neckline. Annalisa's heart pounded a needy rhythm even as she tried to tug herself free of his sensual spell.

'If we marry it will be all right.' His deep voice soothed, almost as hypnotic as his touch. 'Our child will have the protection of my family name.' His thumb traced the line of her collarbone and she trembled. 'You want to protect our child, don't you?'

Annalisa nodded, her throat too dry for speech. The banked heat in his eyes mesmerised her. As did his hand, curling around her neck, fingers sliding into her hair and tugging it down. Her skin prickled deliciously at the sensuous caress against her scalp. She tipped back her head, unconsciously baring her throat. His fingers tightened in her hair and she caught the sultry spice scent of his skin.

That magical feeling was back. Wondrous sensations only Tahir could ignite. Tiny shudders of excitement and pleasure shook her.

'Marriage will protect you both, Annalisa. You'll be safe and cared for.'

She barely heard him over the clamour of her heartbeat. What she felt was so strong surely it was *right*.

'You'll be wealthy and respected, mother of a future monarch. There will be no public backlash or snide remarks about our child. It will be secure and accepted. And you needn't worry I'll interfere or take over your life, apart from the necessary royal obligations. You have everything to gain from our convenient marriage.'

It took an inordinate amount of time for his words to sink in. Annalisa looked up into that proud, stern face and wished she hadn't heard.

She had been melting at his touch, seduced by his tenderness and her need into believing a future with Tahir mightn't be the disaster she'd feared. That perhaps they had something to build on. Something that might flower one day into the sort of love her parents had shared.

Only to discover he wasn't talking about a proper marriage. Her insides caved in as understanding hit. What a fool she'd been, deluding herself.

Convenience was the key word for him, not marriage.

Would they even live together? He'd have lovers; she had no doubt of that. How would she cope? Surely he wouldn't install them in the palace!

Something twisted inside and she hunched reflexively, fearing she'd give in to nausea. She felt hollow, a fragile shell.

Even after Saleem had flayed her with his brutal prejudice, she'd been naïve enough to believe that between she and Tahir there was hope for something precious. Something more than simply escaping sordid scandal.

'Annalisa!' Tahir's voice was sharp with concern.

She ignored him and stumbled to the garden seat, subsiding as the strength ebbed from her shaky legs.

'I'll get a doctor.'

'No!' She tried to gather her wits. 'I'm okay.'

His look told her he didn't believe her. He was poised for instant action.

Wearily she stared up at the man who offered support for her and their child for the sake of respectability. For safety. Possibly even because he feared a public backlash that might affect the monarchy.

But not because he felt anything for her personally.

Annalisa's heart clenched.

Did she have any choice?

Stupid to wish for a real marriage, a loving union, when the only man she cared for wasn't capable of love.

She ignored the pain piercing her. He offered security for her child.

His gaze held hers steadily. His look questioned.

'Very well,' she murmured, finally accepting the inevitable. This was the only option. Anything else was wishful thinking.

Yet still she hesitated, drawing a sustaining breath.

'I'll marry you.' She almost choked on the words.

CHAPTER ELEVEN

'EXCELLENT.'

In an instant he was beside her on the seat. The scent of his skin mingled with fresh salt air and unthinkingly she breathed deep. Behind him stars winked in a black velvet sky. *It should have been a night for lovers.*

'I knew you'd make the sensible decision.'

Sensible. The word was a lead weight. How sensible to marry for public opinion, for show and security? It made a sham of the vows they'd make and all she believed in.

Her melancholy thoughts shattered as Tahir took her hand and bent his head. His lips caressed the back of her hand in a courtly gesture that dragged her straight into another reality. One where the needs of her body and the sentimental hopes he'd just obliterated rose tremulously once more.

No! She'd be a fool to fall for his practised charm.

Yet the sight of his dark head bent over her hand, the pressure of his mouth, ignited feelings she couldn't douse.

She almost sobbed her despair that even now, with her pride and heart in tatters, she responded.

She tugged her hand but his hold tightened.

Her breath hissed as he turned her hand and pressed an open-mouthed kiss to the centre of her palm. To the sensitive spot she hadn't known existed till he'd introduced her to physical pleasure.

Under dark lashes his eyes glittered, bright and knowing.

Her heartbeat accelerated and her fingers itched to stroke his soft hair as she had once before.

Tahir's tongue swirled against her skin and every nerve cell juddered. Bone-melting bliss stole through her.

She opened her mouth to object, but all that emerged was a sigh as floodgates opened on feelings, *needs* she'd struggled so long to suppress.

Where was her resolve? Her strength?

As if attuned to her weakness, Tahir kissed her fingers, the tender skin at her wrist, sending her pulse racing wildly out of control.

This man was dangerous.

She tugged again, surprised when he released her hand. Bright eyes met hers from mere inches away. Fear—or was it excitement?—tugged at her belly as she saw what was in his eyes.

'No, Tahir! I don't—'

The rest was muffled as his mouth claimed hers. Not hard, not recklessly, but with complete assurance. Their lips met, clung, meshed as if it was the most natural thing in the world.

Her hands wedged against his chest. She told herself to push, *hard*. Yet traitorously they clung, fingers spreading greedily across the deep curve of his muscles.

A sob rose in Annalisa's throat. Frustration at his arrogance and her instant capitulation? Or relief at the absolute rightness of it? She'd craved this so long.

Her head spun crazily as he pressed close, his kiss deepening possessively. She tried to fight, to summon strength and detachment, but his passionate mouth, his deft fingers in her hair, were exquisite pleasure.

Once this ended she'd be bereft anyway. Did it matter that for a few glorious moments she succumbed? After this she'd be strong.

She leaned into him, revelling in his fervour, in the seductive power of the one man in the world who awoke her dormant longings.

She heard a growl of approval as her hands crept to his neck. He scooped her up, settling her on his lap. His intimate heat cradled her and excitement spiralled. Her heart galloped at the feel of him surrounding her even as dimly she realised she should stop him.

Tahir didn't even break their kiss. He tucked her close, leaning her back over his arm and claiming her mouth so thoroughly her disjointed thoughts shattered.

Annalisa's fingers tunnelled through his hair as she revelled in a kiss turned hungry and urgent.

Her body throbbed in every secret place.

When his hand slid to the neckline of her dress she arched instinctively. But the tightly sewn bodice defied him and she almost cried out in frustration.

Restlessly Tahir traced the edge of the fabric, testing, then curling his fingers around it. A shocking jolt of excitement shot through her at the idea of him ripping the material, shredding the costly silk and gold so he could caress her bare skin.

She pressed higher, silently urging him.

He cupped her breast, then arrowed in on her peaking nipple. Annalisa groaned as fire flashed. That strange ache was back again between her legs and her body shook.

It was only as she dragged in a deep breath that she realised Tahir had pulled back, ending the kiss to look at her with glittering eyes.

In this light his face seemed pared down to slashing lines. Their gasping breaths drowned the roar of the surf. She shifted and abruptly stilled as she came into contact with proof of his arousal.

His lips tilted in a knowing smile that radiated masculine satisfaction. He lowered his head to her breast.

'No! Don't!' The expression on his face had cut through the glorious haze enveloping her. Harsh reality filtered in. Clumsily Annalisa pushed at his shoulders.

His mouth hovered a breathtaking centimetre from her breast. She shoved harder and he looked up from under raised eyebrows.

'No?' His voice curled around her like rich, dark chocolate. Pure temptation.

What was happening to her? Where was her pride? Her

self-control? He'd decided to kiss her and she'd let him. Shame singed her face.

He doesn't want you. For a couple of hours maybe. When it's 'convenient'.

Was this a test to see how compliant she was?

She gasped down a horrified breath. How easy it would be for him to seduce her into making this relationship more than a paper marriage. If she let him he'd tempt her into surrendering to him physically.

Presumably on the few nights when he preferred less sophisticated amusement in his bed.

Instantly strength returned to her pleasure-drugged body and she shoved harder. This time he straightened.

His eyes narrowed. In the gloom Annalisa caught a glimpse of danger in that stare. For a heartbeat she felt fear, the awareness of the hunted. Then it was gone. Tahir sat back, his hands dropping to the seat. Only the grimness around the lips hinted that she'd displeased him.

Annalisa scrabbled to her feet, reaching for a nearby trellis to keep her upright on weak knees.

'You don't want to kiss me?'

'No!'

His look told her eloquently that she lied.

Stubbornly she stared back. 'That was a mistake.' She wished her voice was steady, without that husky edge. 'I…' She put a hand to her pounding heart and searched for a suitable lie. 'I don't want you to touch me.'

His eyes held hers, as if weighing her mood, her distress. Had he any idea how close she'd come to total capitulation?

'As you wish.'

His words were so unexpected it took her a moment to process them. Could it really be so easy?

She didn't wish! That was the problem. She longed for his touch, his tenderness. For a hint that he felt something for her, even if only a pale reflection of what she still felt for him. Annalisa blinked and looked away to the rolling surf. She *would* master her feelings.

All he felt was lust. And obligation.

'I'll make the wedding arrangements,' he said, with a change of subject that left her floundering. 'You won't have to worry about anything other than resting.'

Could she marry him after what had just happened? Surely this proved he was even more dangerous than she'd thought.

'I'm not sure—'

'Be sure, Annalisa. We *are* marrying.' His tone brooked no argument. 'For the sake of the child.'

For their child. Her shoulders sagged. She had to remember they would be married for her baby, even though her body still thrummed with frustrated desire.

The fact that Tahir had taken her withdrawal so easily just proved he'd been amusing himself. He wasn't really interested. She wasn't his type. Their marriage would be a legality only.

'In the circumstances it will be a small wedding. You won't want the pomp and bother of traditional festivities.'

Annalisa's lips curved in a mirthless smile. If she married the man of her dreams she'd adore a big wedding. But the man of her dreams was a mirage who'd been the centre of her world for a few short days. Now he was no more. The real Tahir had no interest in her except for a light amusement.

'Annalisa? I asked if there's anyone you want to invite.'

She turned to meet his searching look and silently shook her head.

'No one? I know your parents are dead, but isn't there someone to support you?'

'Apart from my uncle?' Annalisa swallowed a clot of bitter regret. 'I'd rather do this alone.' At his steady look she felt compelled to explain. 'I was close to my grandfather but he died recently too. The rest of my family are on the far side of the country. They aren't like Saleem, but…'

But she didn't know how they'd react to her news. Better to break it to them after the wedding.

'My father and I were a team. We were always busy in the community and knew everyone, but there were no really close friends.' Except scientists and scholars scattered around the globe.

At his quizzical look she shrugged. 'There are people I could invite, but no one close. I live in a rural area bound by tradition. It was fine for me to help my father heal people, or represent them by lobbying for services, but I was different. I dress and speak differently. I was allowed freedoms my peers weren't.' She breathed deep. 'For all I was born and bred there, I never fitted in.'

A pang of familiar longing pierced her. The yearning to be wanted and appreciated for herself. Her father and her grand-father had, but they were gone.

'You're alone.' Tahir's voice held a curious note. Not gush-ing sympathy, but an understanding she hadn't expected.

'Hardly alone. I told you I've got cousins galore, all wanting to organise a wedding for me with some local man.' Her words petered out. That was in the past. What would her relationship with them be now?

'And you are marrying a local man.'

'What about you?' She needed to divert her thoughts. 'Will all your family and friends be here for the wedding?' The idea of facing resplendent royal relatives and VIPs petrified her. She was enough of an outsider already.

'Hardly.' The single word held a bitterness so deep she stilled.

'But you're the King,' she prompted, glad to talk about him instead of herself.

'I'm the prodigal, the outsider,' he countered, with a twist of his lips that held no humour. 'I haven't been in Qusay for eleven years. Since my father banished me for scandalous behaviour.'

Banished? She hadn't read that in the press reports.

His father. The father he'd dreamed about. The one Tahir had imagined, in his delirium, beating him.

Surely that had just been a disturbing fantasy? Yet his sombre expression distressed her.

'You didn't know?' he murmured, watching her face so closely she was sure he read her every thought.

'No.' She couldn't imagine being cut off from the people she loved. 'But you must have kept in contact with your family, even if your father…'

At the look on his face her words disintegrated. Hauteur froze his features in an expression of disdain that she hated.

'There was no contact. My brothers didn't know where I was, and I was too busy feeding and clothing myself for a long time to make many long-distance calls. Once I got on my feet there seemed little point. The split was a fact.'

Annalisa's head spun. He'd been exiled and completely alone since…when? Eleven years ago he'd have been only eighteen.

'But you have money.' She gestured helplessly. This didn't make sense. 'The media loves reporting your wealth.'

'Not as much as it loves reporting my misdeeds.' He leaned back and thrust his hand through his dark locks. Suddenly he looked unutterably weary.

'I left with nothing.' He rolled his shoulders as if to relieve an old stiffness. 'I built wealth through luck at the gaming tables, a talent for finance and sheer hard work. I'm sure no one was more surprised or disappointed than my father when I prospered instead of conveniently disappearing or dying.'

It was on the tip of Annalisa's tongue to protest. But what sort of father exiled his son? Or inspired tortured dreams even after eleven years?

She clenched her hands, wanting to reach out and soothe the pain in Tahir's eyes, so at odds with his severe countenance. But she wasn't naïve enough to give in to the impulse. She didn't have the right. He wouldn't thank her for guessing at his hurt.

Annalisa bit her tongue, wondering what else his demeanour of aloof control hid. He was a man of contradictions: demanding, arrogant, abrasive once his memory had returned. His record with women was appalling.

Yet she remembered earlier kindnesses. He'd understood her grief even when she'd fought to stifle it. She remembered his ready sympathy, the dry humour he'd used to lighten her mood when sadness overcame her.

He'd stumbled out of the desert, more concerned for the safety of an animal than himself. He'd treated it with easy kindness, and herself with gentle consideration.

Which was the real Tahir?

Seeing him now, ramrod-straight and wearing an implacable expression of detachment, she was convinced there was more to Tahir than the face he showed the world.

Was it possible the man she'd begun to love in the desert lurked somewhere inside?

Or was that wishful thinking?

'But your mother will be at the wedding,' she murmured, searching desperately for solid ground.

He tensed, his expression stonier than ever. 'I'll invite her. It's up to her whether she chooses to attend.' He paused, then spoke again in a neutral tone. 'My brothers are busy with their own business and their new wives. Rafiq's in Australia and Kareef in Qais. It will be a small wedding. I'll give you details in due course.'

Tahir stood, his tone making it clear their discussion was over. He gestured for her to precede him into the palace.

Her audience with the King was at an end.

'So you enjoyed talking to the guests last night,' Tahir murmured as he accepted tea from his mother.

Rihana's rooms weren't where he'd choose to meet Annalisa, but he didn't trust himself with her in private. Last night she'd looked at him with huge doe eyes and guilt had scored him to the bone.

He couldn't keep his hands off her. He'd kissed her and his good intentions had instantly collapsed. He'd have taken her then and there, on the stone seat! Only the distress in her eyes had stopped him.

He'd have to live with frustration. *Until they were wed.* By then she'd be ready to accept the passion that flared between them and give him what he wanted. What they both wanted.

'Yes.' She watched him warily. She was pale, and dark shadows bruised her eyes. 'The reception was fascinating.'

'What in particular?' Maybe guilt prompted him, but he was curious. Annalisa was such an antidote to the world of cynicism and mistrust he'd known so long.

She shrugged, the movement so jerky he caught his mother's concerned look.

Again guilt speared him. He'd stolen Annalisa's bright future with one greedy lapse of judgement. Trapped himself too, in the yoke of marriage.

A chill filled him at the idea of marrying. He had a deep-seated horror of anything that smacked of commitment. Yet it had to be done. In a couple of weeks, when Annalisa had had time to acclimatise. She looked so fragile.

He'd do his best to support her. After all, in her own way she was as much an outsider as he.

'So many people were interesting,' Annalisa murmured, her husky voice an echo of his erotic fantasies. 'Archaeologists and diplomats. Experts in health and farming.' She stopped, eyes rounding as she caught his gaze, obviously remembering his anger when she'd spoken to that agricultural advisor.

'You find all that interesting?'

'Of course.' He caught a glimpse of the passionate woman who'd entranced him in the desert. 'Don't you?'

'I…' Tahir stopped as something struck him.

He'd been busy learning to be monarch, at the same time working to divest himself of the responsibility but finding no alternative ruler. In all that time he hadn't once been bored. He'd been challenged, frustrated, even occasionally pleased when he'd made important progress.

But never bored.

'Tahir?' Two pairs of eyes stared at him.

Tahir dragged himself back into the conversation, but for the next twenty minutes only half listened.

As he watched Annalisa, so on edge with him, he realised he needed to bridge the chasm he'd created between them. She was wound so tight it couldn't be healthy for the baby or her.

But bridging that gap might leave him vulnerable.

Annalisa made him doubt himself and his certainties.

She made him…feel.

She stirred emotions he wasn't accustomed to. Like last night's jealousy. It had blasted like the desert wind, scouring away his reason. He'd become a covetous brute, lashing out when he should have looked after her.

The reception must have been overwhelming for her. He hadn't missed her wide-eyed look at walls panelled with gold and gems.

He had to protect her and ease her way.

Tahir Al'Ramiz, a champion of duty.

Would wonders never cease?

'What do you think, Tahir?' His mother interrupted his thoughts. 'Will decentralised healthcare get off the ground? Or is it rhetoric?'

He watched Annalisa blush, guessing they'd been expounding upon the problems with the current system. Just the sort of thing she *would* be interested in, he realised with something like pride.

'Since you're interested, come to the next meeting of the working party.'

Silence greeted his suggestion.

'It's not usual,' his mother explained. 'It's normally just officials.'

Didn't he know it? He felt hemmed-in by bureaucracy. It wasn't his style. Ruling a country wasn't his style! But if he was stuck with it, he'd do it his way.

Tahir leaned forward to select a date from the platter before him. He favoured Annalisa with a long look and saw her eyes grow round again. It reminded him of her wide-eyed wonder as their bodies joined. He struggled to find the thread of the conversation.

How did she do that without even trying?

'I'll have one of the secretaries let you both know when the next meeting is.'

'Oh, but I don't think…' Annalisa's words trailed off as he watched her.

'But you *do* think, Annalisa, and that's why I want you there.' Even as he said it he realised how true that was. The meetings had been a tangle of officialdom and little practical input. Besides, it would give Annalisa a chance to think about something other than her pregnancy. He guessed after living a life busy with responsibilities being cooped up here with nothing to do gave her too much time to worry.

'You have experience in healthcare in the provinces. It would be useful to hear your perspective.' He turned to his mother. 'Did you know Annalisa helped provide medical care in outlying villages?'

'I did.' His mother's look might almost have been called approving. He paused in the act of chewing. 'Annalisa would give valuable input. What a good idea.'

Tahir swallowed the date and sat back, his head spinning. His royal mother sounded almost warm in her praise. What was the world coming to?

For as long as he could recall she'd been coolly polite. During his exile she'd refused to answer his calls.

'But I couldn't,' Annalisa murmured. 'I'm not—'

'I'd appreciate your involvement. And my mother will be there.' Tahir leaned forward and fixed Annalisa with a look he knew could melt feminine resolve in under thirty seconds. He watched her blink rapidly as a soft blush warmed her cheeks and throat.

Triumph filled him. She wasn't indifferent, for all her unwillingness to wed.

If he had to marry, he intended to enjoy the benefits. Soon, very soon, she'd give him everything he desired.

CHAPTER TWELVE

TAHIR leaned back in his chair and silently congratulated himself.

With Annalisa's input the working party had achieved more these last couple of weeks than he'd have thought possible. She'd done what his officials hadn't: sought advice from contacts in outlying regions. The plans for coordinated medical care promised to be a success.

His wife-to-be was talented and able. She related to people at all levels, yet was curiously lacking in ego. She was clever, caring, intelligent.

And she aroused him as no other woman.

Even the knowledge that she carried his child couldn't quench his desire. He'd found himself hungrily tracing her figure for some sign of the baby. Instead of shying from the idea, he found her pregnancy evoked urgent, possessive feelings that made his self-imposed distance almost impossible.

The fact that he barely slept, haunted by erotic dreams, was testament to his newfound strength. Once upon a time he'd have seduced her as soon as temptation rose.

Yet he'd found a strange contentment in restraint, knowing he did the right thing, allowing her time to adjust. The way she glowed and her renewed confidence proved he'd done right.

He nodded goodbye to his staff. The room emptied but for Annalisa, still poring over plans.

Silently he paced across to stand beside her.

The familiar wild honey scent of her skin filled his nostrils and sent a tremor through already taut muscles. He inhaled deeply. No scent was more evocative. His hands grew damp as he suppressed the impulse to pull her close.

He watched her graceful movements as she turned the pages. The way she pursed her lips in an unconscious pout. He wanted to bite that succulent bottom lip till she groaned with delight, then plunder her sweet depths. He wanted to see the glitter of incendiary fire in her warm brown eyes as she gasped in pleasure and fulfilment.

He wanted to be with her, possess her, have her smile at him and let him bask in her warmth.

Annalisa sensed Tahir before she saw him. Her hand trembled as she put the papers on the conference table.

Hard fingers clasped her elbow and she froze. Looking up, she sank into the blue depths of Tahir's gaze. Strange that a man with his reputation should have eyes that looked like a glimpse of heaven.

'Come,' he said, drawing her to a group of comfortable chairs. 'Sit with me.'

Automatically she looked back, but the doors were shut. She and Tahir were alone. Heat shimmied through her veins and her palms grew clammy as she remembered what had happened the last time they were alone. Did she trust him? Or herself?

'No one will interrupt,' he assured her. But, seeing the intensity of his gaze, Annalisa didn't feel reassured.

She felt…excited.

Desperately she tried to dredge up horror at her reaction. Yet all she could manage was an edgy sense of playing with fire.

Since the night he'd kissed her she'd been on tenterhooks, fearing he'd tempt her into intimacy. Her nerves were raw, waiting for him to act, and when he didn't she stifled disappointment.

Secretly she'd longed for the marauder who'd entered her bedroom without a by your leave and offered to seduce her. The man who'd only had to kiss her hand to reduce her to trembling need.

He was a puzzle, not easily understood. Yet recently she'd found so much to admire.

Tahir was a born leader who didn't need to bully people into agreement. He had a quicksilver energy that only added to his charisma. And beneath his occasional air of cynicism, despite his reprobate reputation, she suspected Tahir was a decent man.

A man she feared she cared too much for.

Yet he'd left her room that first night in the palace without a qualm. He hadn't touched her after that last searing kiss when she'd agreed to marriage. Clearly whatever allure she'd once held for him was now dead. How could *she*, without an ounce of sophistication, hold his interest?

It scared her that she wanted to.

Annalisa sat on the low divan. To her consternation he sat beside her. Close enough for her to watch his long lashes veil his gaze.

Did he notice her breathing turn shallow? Panic surged at being so close to the man she dreamed of every night, the man she couldn't stop thinking about.

'I've organised a date for our wedding.'

Our wedding.

She swallowed hard and her pulse tripped as she caught the flash of something unsettling in his eyes. Emotions tumbled through her. Relief that he hadn't reneged. Excitement she tried to stifle. Anxiety at whether marriage was the right thing.

'When will it be?' Her voice emerged husky and she reminded herself this was a paper marriage only.

But the way Tahir leaned close, hands engulfing hers, sent other, contrary signals. Fire shot through her veins, warming her all over.

'A week tomorrow.' He paused long enough for her pulse to thud slow and heavy, once, twice. 'Then we'll be man and wife.'

Heat shimmered between them. The sort of heat that ignited each time she allowed herself close to Tahir.

Dangerous heat.

Annalisa sat straighter, trying to look away from his intense gaze. She wanted to jerk out of his hold but feared she'd give away the effect he had on her.

His thumb swept an arc across her hand, sending tremors shooting up her arm. His nostrils flared and a pulse throbbed at his temple, matching the urgent beat in her blood. Deep inside desire woke.

Tahir leaned in and her eyelids flickered. She shouldn't want him to kiss her but she did. So badly.

She struggled for a distraction.

'You've told your mother about the marriage?' Annalisa forced the words out, making one last effort to resist him. 'It's been obvious she doesn't know your plans.'

Obvious Tahir wasn't eager to spread the word he was marrying. Because he didn't really want her. He was stuck with her.

He straightened, looking suddenly more distant.

'Given your hesitation, I thought you'd prefer keeping the engagement private at first.'

Was he serious? 'But she's your mother! She must have wondered what was going on.' Though the relationship between the women had grown close, Annalisa was uncomfortable with her status as a long-standing guest.

'I wished you to stay. That's all she needed to know.'

Annalisa stared. What sort of relationship did he have with Rihana? Nothing like what she'd shared with her father.

'Why don't you like her?' she whispered, then froze, horrified she'd spoken aloud.

His hands clamped round hers and every skerrick of warmth bled from his face.

'I'm sorry. It's none of my business—'

'You've got it wrong.' He paused so long she thought he wouldn't say more. He looked down at her hands clasped in his. His thumb swiped idly across her skin. 'It's my mother who doesn't approve of me.'

His face was a stony mask. Utterly still. Bereft of emotion. Yet she *felt* it, flowing from him, swirling between them.

Pain. Deep, soul-destroying pain.

Annalisa could barely breathe as the weight of his suffering bore down upon her.

Then his face changed. She watched the familiar twist of his lips, the raised eyebrow, the cool eyes. Yet despite his derisive expression she'd swear he looked haunted.

'I'm hardly a model son. I was a disappointment to my parents from an early age.'

Annalisa's heart wrenched at his arrogant attitude, certain it hid suffering.

Fleetingly she remembered he'd worn that same expression on his last morning at the oasis. Had his supercilious behaviour then been a smokescreen too?

She tugged her hands loose from his grip and dared to wrap them in turn around his powerful fists. They were rigid.

'I don't believe that.'

His glare could have frozen water in the desert sun, but she refused to look away. Annalisa didn't understand the need to champion him. She acted on instinct. On emotion so powerful it wouldn't be denied.

'You're hardly in a position to know, my dear.'

The casual endearment was laced with cool dismissal. In response she raised her chin and met him stare for stare.

'I know your mother loves you.'

He jerked beneath her hold. His big shoulders rose and dropped, as if a massive earthquake had thundered through him. An instant later he was still, his look quizzical.

'I appreciate your good intentions. But not all parents are like yours, Annalisa.'

An expression flashed in his eyes. Something so stark it stole her breath and made her more determined to persevere.

'It's there in the way she talks about you.' Annalisa refused to be cowed. 'She talks about you all the time now, did you know that?' At Tahir's amazed look she kept going. 'She talks about all three of you. She's so proud of her sons. Of what strong, honourable men they are.'

Tahir snorted in disbelief and Annalisa grasped his hands tighter, *willing* him to listen.

'It's true. She says you're all different but you have traits in common. Strength, determination, passion, pride. Honour.'

'You're confusing me with someone else.'

She shook her head. 'She said you'd taken on the kingship though you desperately didn't want it. Because you felt obligated.'

Tahir's eyes widened. She pressed on. 'She says that even while you were out of the country you anonymously funded initiatives in Qusay for abused and disadvantaged children.'

'She knew about that?' Another tremor shook his big frame. Annalisa's heart ached. She wanted to reach out and palm his cheek, stroke his hair, soothe him. He looked stunned. Shocked to the core.

Abruptly he dragged his hands from hers, leaving her bereft.

'It's easy to give money when you have a fortune.' A slashing gesture emphasised the words. 'It wasn't important.'

It was on the tip of Annalisa's tongue to say it was important to those who'd benefited from his generosity, but she bit it back.

'So you haven't noticed the way she looks at you? The way she follows your progress around a room?'

It had puzzled her at first, the coolness between mother and son, contrasted with the Queen's avid interest when Tahir wasn't aware of it. Till Annalisa had realised there was an unhealed breach between them.

Tahir's brows furrowed. He opened his mouth, then shut it again.

Finally he shook his head. 'Maybe once she cared. But that stopped long ago.' His voice was clipped, testament to his discomfort. He surged to his feet, looming over her. 'Until I returned to Qusay my mother hadn't spoken to me for years. Not during my exile. Not before.'

His eyes glittered with an ice-cold clarity that chilled Annalisa to the bone. 'She refused even to speak to me the day my father banished me.'

His voice throbbed with a passion that tore at Annalisa's heart.

'So you'll understand why I find it hard to believe you.' He turned abruptly and strode to the door.

Trembling, Annalisa stumbled to her feet. 'I'm not a liar, Tahir. You know that.' She forced the words out over a throat choking at the sight of his torment.

She didn't have explanations, but she was certain Rihana loved her son. If anything, after listening to her discuss her children, she thought Tahir might even be her favourite.

'Maybe you should ask her why she wouldn't talk to you.'

Tahir checked for a moment on the threshold. 'The subject is closed,' he growled. 'I'll hear no more.' He exited, leaving the door hanging open behind him.

He prowled the corridors and courtyards, the antechambers and audience halls. Yet Tahir couldn't shake the words haunting him.

Your mother loves you.

His strides ate up another wing of the palace.

He'd given up believing such platitudes years ago. It no longer mattered. He was a grown man. Had survived on his own—totally, completely on his own—for years.

He didn't need love.

He barely believed in it any more. He'd never had it from his father. And from his mother? He shuddered to a stop. He recalled her warm hugs and tender smiles when he was small. Only when they were alone together. As the years had passed she'd become distant.

Who could blame her? He'd striven to make his father proud. But when it had become clear nothing he did would earn the old man's approval, that in fact his father hated him, Tahir had plunged into excess with an abandon that rivalled even his sire's. Better that than driving himself crazy trying to fathom why the old man detested him.

Had he seen too much of his own weaknesses in his son?

Tahir scrubbed a hand over his face.

He wasn't the sort who inspired or sought love. That was a fool's game. Sentimental folly.

Annalisa imagined things. She was sweet and innocent enough to believe families were about caring.

What stunned him was the way, just for a moment, he'd *wanted* to believe her. He'd craved it with every fibre of his body and what passed for his soul.

He! Tahir Al'Ramiz! The dissolute son of a dissolute father. A man who cared for no one.

Except, he realised, a feisty girl with tender eyes and an indomitable spirit.

He put out a hand to steady himself as the realisation rocked him back on his feet.

He cared…

How long he stood there, unfamiliar sensations swirling through him, he didn't know. *He cared!*

Finally, shaking his head as if clearing it of a waking dream, he looked around and realised he'd stopped outside the dowager Queen's apartments.

Chance? Or a subconscious decision?

Something in his chest gave a queer little jump and his pulse settled into a jagged, staccato beat. He turned to leave, then stopped.

Annalisa's words rang in his ears.

She'd confronted him with a story too unbelievable to countenance. *Surely* it was unbelievable.

Yet eventually he lifted his fist and rapped on the massive door. A voice answered and he forced himself to push the door wide.

His mother looked up from a book. Her eyes met his and just for an instant he saw them sparkle with pleasure. Then, swift as a door slamming, her expression cleared into the familiar one of calm detachment.

Tahir swallowed hard. He stepped inside, his mind whirring.

'Annalisa's not here, I'm afraid.' Her voice was crystal-cool, like the fountains tinkling in the exquisite courtyard outside her chambers. 'If you come later, I'm expecting her for tea.'

'I know.' His voice held an unfamiliar rough edge. He cleared his throat. 'It's you I came to see.'

* * *

Hours passed and Tahir was still in Rihana's rooms.

He felt odd—something like the sensation he'd experienced the first few times his father had used him as a punching bag. As if someone had rearranged his internal organs.

His mother smiled up at him from one of her photo albums and he felt the warmth and wonder of it embrace him.

The albums were filled with photos he hadn't known about. Him on horseback. Him striding down the beach. Him stepping from a four-wheel drive after speeding over the dunes, a rare smile on his teenage features.

Annalisa was right. His mother had cared all along. He'd been too caught up in his bitter struggle against his father to understand how the old man's hatred had affected Rihana and why she'd had to hide her feelings.

He returned her smile, enjoying what he saw in her face and the way it made him feel.

He tried to analyse the sensations and couldn't. He felt too…full, as if all those emotions he'd learned to repress in childhood now pushed too close to the surface. As if it would just take one more tiny scrape of his skin to set them free.

'Mother, I—'

A crash of sound, a deafening boom, rent the air.

Tahir was on his feet before its echo died away. In slow motion he processed the sight of the walls and ceiling dipping and swaying. The decorative lanterns swung impossibly wide.

Memories of a day in Japan that he'd rather forget crowded his brain.

'Earthquake!' He hauled Rihana to her feet, taking in her dazed eyes. 'Quickly, this way.' He half carried her out into her private courtyard.

The initial eruption of sound died, but in the distance he caught an ominous rumbling. Another quake, or a building coming down? Automatically he held Rihana protectively close, well away from the decorative arches lining the courtyard. He scanned the roofline but could see no damage. Could hear no cries for help.

'Stay here,' he ordered. 'Either I or someone else will come for you.'

'Tahir!'

Her urgent tone and her grasp of his sleeve stopped him in mid-stride. He turned. What he saw in her face made him want to stay and comfort her. But he couldn't. Others mightn't be as lucky as they'd been.

'Be careful,' she murmured.

Those two simple words turned his heart over in his chest. He stepped close, gently embraced her and pressed a kiss to her cheek. 'I will. Now, don't forget. Wait here.'

It was the first time he'd kissed his mother in more than a decade.

The news was bad. No damage to the palace, but a section of the old town was devastated. Ancient structures and adobe walls had tumbled into narrow streets, making rescue difficult.

A check on the provinces brought news that only the capital was damaged. Nevertheless, Tahir set in motion national arrangements for evacuation should there be aftershocks.

Rescue and medical teams worked at full stretch. Tahir had contacted his cousin, Zafir, once King of Qusay and now ruler of nearby Haydar, and arranged for more rescue specialists to fly in. Tahir's brother, Kareef, had already sent men from the mountains of Qais to help.

As afternoon faded into night Tahir was still busy directing, reassuring, planning. He did it on autopilot. Beneath his calm façade lay a fear so potent it froze his bones and threatened to paralyse his brain.

Annalisa was missing.

Just thinking it sent dread spiralling through him.

Every centimetre of the palace and grounds had been searched. Surrounding streets had been investigated.

Had she gone home, angry after their last encounter?

Guilt lanced him. Even as he pored over city plans with engineers and officials he was alert for footsteps, lest one of his staff return with news of her. He hoped for and feared it.

It was his fault she'd gone. He'd barked at her, furious that she'd dared to pry into the most private part of his life. He'd punished her for trying to heal the rift between himself and his mother.

His stomach churned at the knowledge that he was to blame for her disappearance.

Silently he told himself over and over that she wouldn't have ventured into the old *souk*. But he didn't believe his own reassurances. He wanted to scour the streets himself, looking for her.

Already he'd been down amongst the wreckage too often for his staff's liking, hoping to find her. They'd protested he was in danger. Only the knowledge he was more useful coordinating the rescue efforts had kept him in the makeshift emergency centre on the edge of the damage zone.

The acrid scent of fear filled his nostrils with every breath. His heart drummed frantically.

Never had he felt so powerless. If anything happened to her…

He'd rather endure a lifetime of beatings than this. Waiting, trying to be strong for those needing his leadership, while terror gnawed at his vitals. If only he had some clue where she'd gone.

He'd thought himself safe in his isolated world, relying on no one, caring for nothing.

What he felt now obliterated that self-deception.

Finally he gave in to those urging him to rest for an hour before daybreak. But instead of returning to the palace he prowled the streets. People welcomed their King's presence. But it was the need to find Annalisa that kept him going.

He'd almost given up hope when he came upon a temporary triage centre on the furthest side of the disaster zone. Makeshift awnings protected the wounded and lights were set up to assist the medics.

Movement caught his eye: a spill of rich dark hair. Golden highlights glinted as the woman turned her head. Impatiently she reached round and secured the waist-length tresses in a familiar gesture.

Tahir felt a huge weight rise to block his throat and impair his breathing. He strode through the debris, past stretchers, piles of rubble and huddled figures. He heard nothing but the rush of blood in his ears.

As he approached she turned, her hand out to grasp a nearby pole for support. Her clothes were rumpled and dirty. A dark stain marred her shirt.

Terror jammed his throat as he realised it was blood.

She stumbled and he ran, just in time to scoop her off her feet before she fell.

Tahir's heart pumped out of control as his arms closed convulsively around her. She felt warm and wonderful and alive. Alive. Thank God.

He was whirling around, looking for a doctor, when her voice finally penetrated.

'Put me down. I have work to do.'

'Work?' He stared down into her exhausted face, terrified at the intensity of what he felt.

'I'm helping the wounded. You have to let me go.'

'You're injured.' He shouldered through the crowded space towards a couple of doctors bent over a patient.

'It's not my blood, Tahir. Tahir?'

But he was already talking to a white-haired medic who explained Annalisa had been here all night, helping.

Even then Tahir couldn't release her. He listened as if from a distance as the doctor reassured him that she was unharmed, heard praise for her efforts. But he couldn't trust himself to believe.

Blind instinct urged him to ignore the expert's words and Annalisa's urgings. He needed her close.

'You need rest,' he said as her voice grew strident. 'You're pregnant, remember?'

His words fell into a pool of silence. The emergency staff, patients, even his staff who'd followed him seemed to still.

Then the doctor was agreeing, saying she'd done enough and urging Annalisa to go. They were closing this centre anyway and moving to the hospital.

Tahir instructed his staff to help pack up. He'd be back

soon. His stride lengthened as he passed into the wider streets of the new city.

'Tahir?' She didn't sound angry now. 'You can put me down. I'm fit and healthy. Honestly.'

But he walked on, arms tight as steel as he cradled her close. He didn't want to let her go. He wouldn't let her go.

He looked into worried dark eyes, saw a flush stain her lovely face, the pout of concern on her lush mouth.

Tahir remembered the terror of losing her. The sense of loss. The fear he'd never find her. Horror still trickled through his belly at the recollection.

Realisation struck him with the force of an act of a divine power.

He couldn't let her go.

The man who'd turned independence into an art form, self-reliance into a way of life, had met his match.

He needed her.

CHAPTER THIRTEEN

IT WAS late in the day when Annalisa woke. She'd fallen exhausted into bed. Yet she hadn't slept for hours. Instead she'd replayed events in her mind. The quake, her work to help the wounded.

And Tahir, appearing out of nowhere and sweeping her into his arms. Her heart fluttered at the memory.

He'd been a stranger: intent, focused, all hard-muscled strength and determination. No hint of the playboy, just one hundred percent powerful, commanding male. One look at the set of his jaw had told her she hadn't a hope of escaping his hold. *Even if she'd wanted to.*

In his embrace was exactly where she'd wanted to be.

She'd been so worried for him, but had found herself in the thick of disaster and hadn't been able to turn her back on the pitifully wounded victims.

Tahir had barely heard her as he'd marched through the dark streets. Nor had he relinquished his hold when he'd reached his vehicle. He'd held her tight all the way, then carried her through the palace to her rooms.

Ignoring propriety, he'd only released her when he reached her bed. Even then he'd loomed close as servants scurried to provide food and run her a bath.

He'd looked immovable, his features a study in potent masculinity as he stared silently down at her.

Something had stretched taut between them. A tension she

hadn't been able to name but had felt with every slow breath, every tingle of awareness across her burning hot skin and in the deep, slow, coiling excitement in her belly.

When a maid had announced the bath was ready he'd abruptly disappeared, leaving her to ponder what had just happened.

When Tahir looked at her that way her doubts melted into nothing. It was like the sizzle in the air the night they'd made love. But more. Something stronger still.

Was she a fool, reading too much into his actions? Had he just been protecting his unborn baby?

And yet…she found herself hoping it was more.

She turned from her view of the sun setting in a blaze of colour. It was time to—

Annalisa's footsteps faltered as she spied the figure just inside her room. His hand clenched high on the filmy curtains that separated the entry foyer from her chamber.

'Tahir?' Her husky voice betrayed her longing.

Need rose. It had gnawed at her so long. A need that had escalated last night as he'd carried her with the stern certainty of a man claiming his woman.

She *wanted* him to claim her. *She wanted to be his.*

Every warning, every doubt, ebbed in the face of her feelings for Tahir. She'd tried to focus on the negative, to tell herself she shouldn't care for a man who didn't love her. But stern logic didn't work any more.

Flutters of excitement whirled and swooped in her abdomen. She stroked trembling fingers down the opalescent silk of the gown Rihana had given her.

His gaze followed the movement.

Heat blossomed low in her womb and at the apex of her thighs. She tried to calm herself and failed.

Last night's crisis had cut through her attempts to be sensible and careful. All that remained was raw feeling.

What she felt for Tahir was stronger than ever.

He was the embodiment of every dream she could no longer deny. Tall, suave and potently masculine in dark trousers and a black shirt, his head bare.

Tension radiated from him. His jaw was rigid, his face composed of taut angles and lines. His eyes blazed like the sky at midday. Almost too bright to watch. Yet she couldn't look away.

She took a step towards him and his hand clenched white-knuckled on the gossamer fabric. Her heart thumped out of kilter at what she read in his expression.

He looked fierce, stern, forbidding. Yet she felt no fear. For there was warmth too. Such warmth.

Surely it was real, not a product of her needy imagination?

For so long she'd wanted him to want her, really want *her*, as she did him. Now she had her wish. The force of that look almost buckled her knees.

Instinctively she realised he battled with himself. She had so little experience yet at some primitive level she understood her power over him.

For he had the same power over her. He'd wielded it from the first. She'd been blind to think she could escape its pull. Foolish to think she could walk away.

They might be king and commoner but in this they were equals. That knowledge gave her strength.

'Tahir?' Her voice was a barely audible throb of sound.

His fingers eased their grip on the fabric and his arm dropped to his side. He hefted a breath that inflated his chest and lifted his shoulders. It shuddered from him in a sigh. Annalisa felt its twin tremble through her.

He stepped forward, his long stride closing the distance between them. All she saw was him.

'Habibti.' My darling. His deep voice was hoarse and unfamiliar. The sound of his endearment crept like warm fingers up her spine till she shivered, her nipples peaking.

This close, she saw the lines of fatigue around his eyes. Had he been up all night and all day too?

Annalisa opened her mouth to ask about the rescue, but he reached out and pressed his index finger to her lips. She inhaled the warm scent of man, of Tahir, and heat pooled low in her body. She felt herself tremble on the brink of a precipice. No thought now of their turbulent past. The emotion she'd read in his ravaged features last night was more important than what had gone before.

For countless moments they stood, drawn by a force so strong the air crackled with it.

The tension was too much to bear. Annalisa swayed towards him. A muscle in his jaw worked; his eyes devoured her.

Tentatively she lifted her hand, unable to stop herself. She needed to feel him, safe and real.

Before she could touch him he hauled her close, slamming her into his rigid body. His arms wrapped hard round her, tucking her against him as if he had no intention ever of releasing her.

Annalisa trembled as his fiery heat encompassed her. Beneath her ear his heart thudded, matching her own racing pulse. She hugged him close, squeezing tight as tears she didn't even understand stung her eyes.

A hiccough escaped as she fought back surging emotion that threatened to overwhelm her.

Long fingers cupped her chin and tilted her face up. Then Tahir was kissing her, lips slanted across her mouth in stormy possession. He gave no quarter, allowed no hesitation, as he took her.

He delved deep, kissing her thoroughly, like a conquering marauder taking his fill. Yet there was a piercing sweetness to his caress that spoke of far more than easy gratification. Her heart soared at his urgency and underlying tenderness.

His hands shook as he cupped her face. For all his power and physical strength, Tahir was as needy as she.

Annalisa answered his kisses with her own, leaning on tiptoe and planting her hands in his thick, soft hair, as if to prevent him pulling away.

Tahir groaned deep in his throat as she slid her tongue into his mouth, mimicking his caresses, luxuriating in the dark mutual pleasure consuming them.

He bowed her back over his arm, his legs wide around hers as he demanded even more. Gladly she gave it, sinking into a warm tide of delight as their open-mouthed kiss grew needier, deeper, hungrier. *This* was what she'd craved.

A barely familiar throb quickened in the place between Annalisa's legs and she shifted restlessly, finding comfort in the press of his body against hers.

The pressure inside rose and she kissed him feverishly. She needed him closer even than this.

A moment later she was falling, and the air was squeezed from her lungs as he came down on her, pressing her into the cushioned mattress of her low bed.

Eyes wide now, she saw him prop himself on one arm, keeping most of his weight off her. Her eyes met his and thought fled.

Such fierce passion in his sky-blue eyes. Annalisa only had to meet his look and she spiralled towards paradise.

'Tahir.' Every scintilla of longing and hope and tremulous desire was in that one word. And she didn't care. All she cared about was having this one man who meant so much, here where he belonged. For this time it was right.

Her body softened, accommodating his hard length, readying for his possession.

A shudder racked his big frame and she saw the tendons in his neck stretch taut. Tenderness filled her at his vulnerability.

'I had to come. I need…' He shook his head, eyes squeezing shut.

She felt a spasm of sympathy clench her heart, seeing his inner turmoil, feeling the same driving force for intimacy.

'I need too, Tahir.'

At her whispered admission his eyes snapped open. Cerulean fire blazed down, scorching her face, her lips.

'*Habibti.*' The endearment was a low hum of sound that curled up and wrapped itself around her, warming every last recess of her body. Emotion shimmered in each syllable.

He lay poised above her as her heart thudded out a rhythm that spoke of desire, need, love. A love she could no longer deny for this proud, complex man.

Acknowledging her love didn't scare her when she saw Tahir at the mercy of his own emotions. Not just desire but tenderness, relief and regret. She recalled the stark fear on his face last night, the convulsive clamp of his arms around her, and wanted to soothe the remnants of his anxiety away.

She raised her hands to his face, to the strong jaw so smooth it must be freshly shaved. Over high cheekbones, feathering his brow, his ears, his nose and lips. She learned his face as a blind woman would, committing each detail to memory.

His tongue sleeked across her palm and she stilled. He clasped her hand to his mouth and kissed her there, laving and nipping and caressing till longing bubbled up inside and burst out in a throaty moan of bliss.

Then he was gone, rolling off her and leaving her bereft and wanting. Instinctively she turned towards him, but already he'd moved. He knelt, hands skimming up her legs, drawing the delicate silk she wore higher and higher.

Excitement rose as their gazes meshed. She lifted her bottom so he could push the fabric up. Then he peeled the dress over her shoulders and head, tossing it in a stream of pearly colour across the room.

Movement ceased as he loomed above, straddling her hips. His chest heaved, straining the buttons of his shirt. His gaze roved greedily.

A twinge of self-consciousness penetrated Annalisa's heady pleasure. Had her waist thickened? Her breasts seemed fuller. Too full? Instinctively she lifted her hands to shield herself, but he clamped hold of her wrists and pulled her arms wide.

She *felt* his eyes on her skin, like the graze of flesh on flesh. Tiny explosions erupted within her. Excitement reached fever-pitch just at the way he devoured her with his eyes. Her breasts seemed to swell against the lace of her bra and between her legs she felt dampness.

She revelled in his breathless regard. The way he looked at her made her feel like the most important being on the planet.

Deliberately he bent and planted a kiss to her belly, where her womb cradled the tiny new life they'd made.

Annalisa's heart turned over, undone by the reverence and tenderness of the gesture. She slipped her hands free to cup his head in her hands, cradling him to her as a flood of emotion stole her heart.

Seconds later he was moving, slipping off her bra and panties with an ease that reminded her just how practised he was with women.

Yet even that knowledge didn't give her pause. Not now. *This was meant to be.*

She welcomed his caressing hands, shifting under each sweep of his palm, each circling finger. She gasped as he bent his dark head to suckle at her breast, gently at first, then, as she held him close, tugging greedily, in a way that sent shafts of fire arrowing through her.

His hand slipped down, restlessly stroking her hip, her thigh, the secret needy place where his touch sent waves of pure pleasure rushing through her.

Annalisa's heart raced. Her skin bloomed, flushed with sexual arousal and a soaring happiness she'd never known. Her hips lifted off the bed, towards Tahir's caress. Yet he took his time, pleasuring her slowly, as if eking out every nuance of delight.

'Please, Tahir,' she gasped. 'I want…'

Hooded eyes met hers. She drank in the sight of his desire-ridden face just centimetres from the peak of her breast. Dark burnished golden skin beside pale.

Her proud lover.

A tremor shook her, and another.

'Then take what you want, *habibti*.' He ripped open his shirt and tossed it aside, revealing his powerful torso. A moment later he shoved his trousers and underwear off and onto the floor. His feet were bare, and she had no idea if he'd come to her like that or shucked off his footwear beside the bed.

Her throat dried as he stretched out beside her, propped on one arm. He looked utterly relaxed, like some long, lithe predator, resting in the heat of the day. Only the rapid rise and fall of his powerful chest gave him away. And his jutting erection.

Her eyes rounded as she took in the glory of Tahir, fully

aroused. How could she have forgotten his sheer magnificence? Or had she been so overwhelmed by her first experience of lovemaking that she hadn't looked? This time she felt no nerves, no anxiety. Just love and a soul-deep need.

His erection throbbed as she watched. 'See what you do to me?' His voice sounded curiously tight, as if he were in pain.

Her eyes roved him and hunger grew. She reached for him, curling fingers tentatively around his surprisingly soft skin. Warm silk over iron, over pure potent masculinity.

Something plunged deep inside her and she moved nearer.

His hand closed around hers, prying her fingers loose and then dragging her hand wide, to his other side, as he rolled onto his back. He held her like that, poised over him, holding her more with the searing intensity of his eyes than with his touch on her hand.

'Take what you want,' he repeated. This time the words were so slurred she wouldn't have understood if she hadn't been watching his face.

Did he mean…?

She looked down to where their bodies touched. A frisson of erotic awareness raced through her. She sank against him a fraction and his mouth tightened in a grimace that she understood too well. The pulse throbbing between her legs was a driving force, urging her to take as well as give.

Carefully Annalisa pushed herself onto her knees so she could straddle his supine form. His heavy weight between her legs, pushing against her thigh, sent a shudder of anticipation through her. As did the gleam in Tahir's eyes.

When his hands closed around her waist, adjusting her position above him, she let him, eager to ease the burgeoning ache inside.

A second later she felt pressure where she most needed it as Tahir rose beneath her. He drew her inexorably down, meanwhile pushing higher and higher, till surely any more was impossible.

One final sharp thrust of his hips and he lodged deep within her, part of her. The magic of it stunned her. She felt full, but not just physically. Her heart welled with the intensity of her emotions. With love for Tahir.

'All right?'

She nodded, bereft of speech as he massaged her breasts and sent delight coiling. He shifted beneath her, slowly at first, then to an increasing tempo that made the most of the friction between their shifting, sliding bodies.

Annalisa leaned forward, her hands on his shoulders, falling into the depths of his welcoming eyes. Long fingers clamped her hips, holding her firm against him as he thrust higher, harder.

Then with a hoarse cry she was flying, soaring above the world in exquisite delight as fire shimmered in her veins and pleasure exploded. An instant later Tahir shuddered beneath her, within her, as he gasped her name.

Greedily he hauled her close and they rode the last rocketing paroxysms together, his musky, hot skin fragrant against her, his heart pounding in tempo with hers, his body enfolding her.

Annalisa breathed deep of pleasure and peace and knew this was where she belonged. With Tahir. Always.

The white heat of cataclysmic orgasm burned Tahir's retinas. Scorched his flesh. Seared his soul.

He wrapped Annalisa closer, tangling his hand in her long hair, catching her slim leg with his knee, locking them together as if to prevent her moving.

He couldn't let her go.

He'd been right last night. *He needed Annalisa.*

Sex had never been so good. But he knew now this was more than physical satisfaction.

Tahir couldn't put a name to it. Couldn't get his mind to grapple with definitions and meanings.

But she was his. By right of conquest. By her own choice. By dint of the simple fact he'd never release her.

He'd never needed a woman as he needed Annalisa.

He'd never *needed* any woman.

He nuzzled her neck, breathing deep of her sweetness. Instantly tendrils of desire coiled within him, tightening sinews and hardening flesh.

Blood roared in his ears and rushed south. He stroked her collarbone, let his fingers trail to her breast and felt her shiver.

It was too soon. It shouldn't even be possible, not yet. But there was no mistaking the stirring in his loins.

Tentatively he moved, still lodged inside her.

He felt her grip on his shoulders tighten, reminding him how she'd scored his flesh in the throes of ecstasy. The idea of her marking him was strangely pleasing.

'Tahir?'

He shifted so he could see her, read the surprise and confusion in her flushed face. He stroked a strand of hair from her face. 'Too soon?'

Wide eyes held his for a moment, then a tiny dimple appeared in her cheek as she smiled and shook her head.

That was all the encouragement he needed. Moments later she was on her back, her hair a glossy fan beneath her as he took her slowly, tenderly and thoroughly.

This time he kissed her all the while, swallowed her small mews of pleasure and surprise, cupped her face in his hands as she gasped her completion. Mere seconds later the fire rose in him, spreading from his groin to his belly, sending incendiary flares through his whole body and setting a blaze in his lungs that made him gasp for breath.

He burned for her till the explosion blew him apart.

Yet even then the fire kept burning inside, a permanent unquenchable glow.

Tahir slid into oblivion, basking in its warmth, his arms locked about her.

CHAPTER FOURTEEN

'WHAT are these scars?' A gentle finger traced across the small of his back. 'Was it an accident?'

Tahir stilled in mid-stretch, tensing instinctively. In the past when women had asked that he'd brushed off the query, pretending the marks didn't matter. Yet each time the truth had burned his soul like red-hot coals.

The reminder of his father's 'loving' touch. Though Tahir couldn't see the scar tissue, it was a permanent brand of who he was and what his past had been.

It would be easy to demur now, to hide the shame of his past. But he didn't want to lie to Annalisa. For the first time he wanted to unburden himself. To share just a little. The realisation made his stomach clench in fear.

His reprobate reputation hadn't scared Annalisa. Nor had his position. She'd stood up to him time and again. She didn't act like any other woman he knew.

She acted as if she cared.

His mind shied from the notion even as its allure drew him. After a lifetime of believing himself unlovable, the idea of someone caring about him was too foreign.

Yet she'd been right about his mother.

'I'm sorry. I didn't mean to pry.'

'No.' He cut off her hurried apologies. 'It's all right.' He turned, and her gentle smile filled him with such pleasure it gave him the impetus to continue.

'It's a mark from a lash.'

'A lash?' Her brow furrowed in confusion, her eyes clouding, and Tahir was assailed by doubt.

He couldn't taint her with knowledge of his sordid past. The desire to talk about it was mere selfish weakness.

He rose quickly from the bed, only to feel her hand on his arm, stopping him.

Looking down, he met her questioning gaze head-on. Her expression was clear, open.

It reminded him of her extraordinary inner strength. The strength she'd needed to nurse him with no assistance in the desert. The strength to stand up to the man who was her sovereign and refuse to comply with his wishes.

For all her innocence, Annalisa was a strong woman.

'Tell me. Please?'

Finally he sank back onto the rumpled sheets and let her slip her arms about him. She leaned her head on his shoulder and her long hair blanketed him. He loved the feel of her near. It filled him with emotions he'd never felt and gave him strength to admit what he'd never told a soul.

'It's from my father's whip. He used to beat me regularly.'

So it hadn't been just Tahir's delirium. The beatings had been real. She'd wondered, but hadn't wanted to believe.

Her pulse pounded sickeningly. Not one beating but regularly. Not just with fists, but a whip. What sort of sadist behaved so?

Annalisa choked on rising bile.

Suddenly Rihana's comment about Tahir contributing to charities for abused children made perfect, horrible sense. Had he tried to save others from what he'd suffered?

Annalisa clasped him tight. She wished she'd been able to protect the boy who'd grown into this reserved man. Was it any wonder he hid his inner self? Or that he was difficult to know?

Fiercely she hugged him, sensing his unwillingness to talk.

'Don't cry, *habibti*.' He brushed her wet cheek where it pressed into his shoulder. 'It was a long time ago.'

'But you still remember it, all these years later. You still bear the scars.' They both knew she wasn't talking about the marks on his back. 'In the desert you dreamed about it every night.'

He wrapped an arm around her and she snuggled in, grateful for his acceptance. Tahir was unused to sharing anything more than his body. He was the sort of man to keep confidences to himself.

Had he ever talked of this before?

'I survived.' His tone was flat and uncompromising.

'You did more than survive,' she whispered urgently. 'You put it behind you. Look at you now.'

'Don't glamorise me, Annalisa.' His tone was sharp. 'Just because I'm Sheikh of my people it doesn't make me a good man.'

'No. But you *are* a good man.' She thought of his care for her at the oasis when grief had engulfed her. His anonymous efforts to improve the lives of children. The sensible, caring way he'd taken up the reins as ruler of a kingdom, though he didn't want the crown. The efficient way he'd mobilised every resource into a rescue effort after the quake, maintaining calm with his presence. The fact that he would marry her to make things right for their child.

'Hardly that.' His laugh was short and harsh. 'I'm too like my father. I've spent years wallowing in pleasure, seeking instant gratification, building a reputation for self-indulgence.'

'You're not like him.' She bridled at the notion. 'You're not manipulative or cruel.'

'Maybe only marriage and fatherhood will bring out my true depths.'

Annalisa reared back, staring aghast into his grim face, hearing his hollow tone. Was he serious? He surely couldn't fear that?

She'd seen him at his lowest ebb, on the edge of death, stripped of every pretence. The man she'd known then, the man she knew now, was nothing like the monster he tried to paint himself. The arrogant cynic wasn't the true Tahir.

She levered herself onto her knees and rose till their faces were level. She cupped his face in her palms and met his searing gaze.

'You're nothing like that—do you hear me?' Her voice rose with a potent fury she barely understood. 'I've never heard such rubbish in my life. Don't you *ever* speak like that again, or I'll know you're just after sympathy.'

His eyes widened in astonishment, as if the kitten he'd petted had turned into a tigress and drawn blood.

'You can't use that excuse to hide from life.'

'You don't know what you're talking about.' Before her eyes his expression chilled, became all arrogant hauteur.

'And you're too old not to face the truth.'

Her heart slammed against her ribs, fear rising that she'd pushed him too far. But the thought of him imagining himself like his brutal father was unbearable.

'Why did he beat you?' she asked before he could respond. 'Did he beat your brothers too?'

For a long time she thought Tahir wouldn't answer. His mouth thinned to a grim line and his eyes flashed with a mix of emotions. Her hands tightened on his jaw and, seeing his turmoil and pain, she couldn't stop herself leaning forward and pressing a tender kiss on his lips.

Would it be the last time he let her kiss him?

Fear catapulted through her as she realised she wanted more than anything to spend her life with Tahir. But perhaps she'd pushed him so far he'd turn his back on her.

Warm hands framed her face. Gentle thumbs scraped fresh tears from her cheeks as he drew back a fraction.

'I told you,' he murmured gruffly, 'not to cry. That's a royal command.' His mouth tilted in the lopsided smile that flipped her heart in her chest. 'I don't like it.'

Shakily Annalisa nodded, swallowing a knot of emotion.

He hadn't pushed her away. Instead his hands were gentle as they shaped her face.

'You're not going to give up, are you?'

She shook her head, her long hair swirling around her bare shoulders in a reminder that she was naked. They were both naked. But it didn't matter. Not when she saw pain shadowing Tahir's eyes.

With a sigh he lifted her up, right off her knees, and sat her on his lap, warm flesh against warm flesh. He reached for a coverlet and dragged it over her, cocooning them together under its satin comfort, hugging her close. His chin rested on her head and his heart thudded strong and familiar beneath her ear.

'No, he didn't beat Kareef and Rafiq,' he murmured at last. 'Just me.'

'But why?' Surely abusers weren't so discriminating?

Silence for another thirty seconds. 'I spent a lifetime wondering that, thinking it was a fault in me that provoked his hatred. My earliest memories are of his rage, his disapproval.' He paused. When he continued his voice was flat. 'It was because he thought I wasn't his son.'

Annalisa jerked in his hold, stunned. 'Seriously?'

He nodded. 'Oh, yes. After all these years my mother has finally explained what she didn't dare before.'

His chest expanded in a deep breath.

'My parents had an arranged marriage. My father amused himself with mistresses but he was incredibly jealous of his wife. She had a difficult birth with Rafiq, and on her doctor's recommendation she spent several months in France, recuperating. When someone made a sly remark about how she'd enjoyed herself with friends my father decided she'd taken lovers. It wasn't true, but that made no difference.'

Tahir tugged Annalisa close and she shut her eyes, grateful for his warmth as she imagined Rihana's life with a cruel brute who didn't love her.

'Then when I was born I was different. I didn't have the pale ice-blue eyes of his family. I stood out from him and my brothers.'

She stiffened, staring at his wide shoulder before her. 'Your father didn't think you were his son because your eyes were a darker blue?'

Tahir shrugged and she felt his muscles ripple. 'He wasn't a reasonable man. He was unhinged on the subject. My mother even suggested a DNA test, but he was paranoid news of it would leak. His pride wouldn't countenance anyone knowing he might have been cuckolded.'

He paused, breathing deep. 'It was no wonder I couldn't please him no matter how I tried. He didn't publicly accuse me of being a bastard. That would have reflected on his ability to keep his wife under control. Instead he made my life hell.'

'He made you his whipping boy.'

'Literally.' There was no humour in his laugh.

'And your mother?'

'No, he didn't beat her.' Tahir must have read her mind. 'He realised he could exact a more exquisite revenge by maltreating me and letting her know she was helpless to stop it.' His hand tightened on her shoulder. 'He'd shown his displeasure from the first, and she soon learnt that if she showed affection to me I'd pay for it.'

'How she must have suffered.' Annalisa shuddered at the idea of being unable to protect her own child. Short of running away and leaving her elder sons to the mercy of a vicious father, under traditional Qusani laws Rihana had had little power to stop it.

'I never realised how much,' Tahir murmured, 'till you forced me to talk to her.'

'Forced you? I—'

'I'm grateful, Annalisa, believe me.' His hand slipped down her arm in a slow caress that made her melt against him. 'If you hadn't brought up the subject I'd never have confronted my mother and known the truth.'

Annalisa luxuriated in his approving tone as much as in the sensation of chest hair and solid muscle beneath her cheek.

Grateful… It wasn't love, but surely it was a start.

'For years I thought she didn't care.' His voice was husky. 'Now I know she distanced herself from me because any sign of love on her part provoked more furious retribution for me. She tried to protect me the only way she could.'

His hold on her tightened.

'I was petrified he'd begin physically abusing her after I was exiled, but even then she wouldn't break her silence.' He paused, his breath fast and loud. 'She feared he'd kill me if she returned my calls. He knew I'd tried to contact her again and threatened violent retribution if she spoke to me.'

'Tahir!' Annalisa clung close, her arms tight around his torso. 'That's monstrous!'

She felt him shake his head above her. 'He *was* a monster. The damage he did.' Tahir stroked the hair back from her brow. 'Even when he died my mother didn't call me. She thought she'd killed my feelings by seeming to turn her back on me. She was afraid *I* didn't care for *her.*'

When all the time it had been the other way around. Tahir had believed his mother hadn't loved him.

What would that do to a child?

Annalisa's heart cracked even as fierce maternal protectiveness surged at the notion of anyone abusing *her* child like that.

Now she understood Rihana's words. Tahir had had everything he wanted: success, wealth, women. But not the one thing he'd really craved.

Love.

Tahir had been without love, or believed himself without it, most of his life.

Jagged fear shot through her. He'd found pleasure and comfort in her body. Yet he'd committed himself only to a marriage of convenience. Would Tahir accept the one thing she wanted most of all to give him?

Would he accept her love?

He'd spent so long cultivating his independence and his self-belief as a man unworthy of deep regard, maybe he was no longer able to accept love or even believe in it.

Was he capable of reciprocating? Of loving her?

Annalisa found her answer the next day.

After a night of passion beyond anything she'd believed possible, after tenderness that brought tears to her eyes more than once, Tahir left.

Words of love trembled on her tongue, her heart so full she had to share her feelings.

Yet he looked so weary after another night without sleep.

His expression settled into grim lines as he spoke of the need to oversee the rescue efforts and she didn't have the heart to burden him with more.

Others needed him more urgently. Her news, her needs, could wait a little longer.

Besides, she shied from the possibility he'd freeze when he heard her admission.

Perhaps he'd reject her. She wasn't ready for that.

Her love for him had grown so much, obliterating her doubts once she saw beneath the mask he presented the world. She wanted to stay and make him happy. Prove to him love was possible and that they could have far more than a marriage of convenience. That they could make a family together.

She was so preoccupied it took her a while to realise the stir she caused as she moved through the palace much later in the day. Everyone looked at her differently, from servants to officials and visitors waiting for appointments.

Overnight the news of where Tahir had spent the night must have spread. Or perhaps it was the way he'd blurted out news of her pregnancy in public.

People refused to meet her gaze, bowing lower than ever as she passed, yet she felt their eyes on her back. Heat crawled up her throat and into her cheeks as she entered an audience chamber to be greeted by a cessation of all conversation. No doubt they'd been gossiping about the latest royal scandal, confirmed by the Sheikh himself.

Stiffening, her pulse thudding, Annalisa paused, grateful that she'd again worn one of the beautiful gowns Rihana had pressed on her. She might feel small and insignificant, but at least she looked as if she belonged in this world of wealth and finery.

She lifted her chin, forcing down the impulse to spread her hand over her abdomen in a telltale protective gesture.

Did they assume she was simply the latest in the long series of Tahir's conquests?

Her stomach plunged. Remembering how he'd left so abruptly, and his air of distraction, maybe they were right. Was she kidding herself that Tahir could feel more for her than duty and physical pleasure?

He'd shared some of his past but that didn't mean he loved her.

Yet she refused to give up her dreams without a fight. She owed it to her baby too, to try and build a meaningful marriage.

Turning on her heel, she spun round and marched to Tahir's offices. His senior private secretary was alone in the outer office.

'Excuse me,' she said, approaching his desk. 'I wonder if you can help me with some information?'

'Of course.' He stood abruptly, his expression uncomfortable as he shot a glance towards the other office.

Instantly a premonition hit Annalisa. A feeling of impending disaster. These last weeks she'd developed an easy relationship with Tahir's staff. What had changed?

The secretary's eyes dipped fleetingly to her waist and her poise almost crumbled. Of course. News of her pregnancy and a potential scandal changed everything.

Warily she let him lead her towards a private sitting room partly screened from the main area.

Her lips twisted bitterly. Was she such an embarrassment she had to be ushered from sight?

'I'd like you to look up the King's appointments,' she said as they walked, her voice a little too strident as she fought embarrassment and anger. 'We're marrying next week and I need details of the time and location so I can arrange some invitations.'

If she was going to fight for Tahir, attempt to turn this into a real marriage, she'd start as if it were real. She'd proudly invite her family. Every last cousin. She refused to let Tahir turn their wedding into a hole and corner affair, as if he were ashamed of her.

The secretary halted so abruptly Annalisa almost walked into him.

'I'm sorry,' he muttered. 'Pardon me.' He turned but didn't meet her eyes. 'Won't you take a seat?'

She shook her head, watching with growing concern the way he clasped and unclasped his hands, clearly ill at ease.

'No, thanks. I'd rather stand. Now, about the wedding?'

He swallowed hard, as if clearing a constriction in his throat. Still he didn't look her full in the face.

'I'm sorry, I…' He paused, looking back to the office as if seeking help.

'You were saying? Just the time and location will do.'

'I'm afraid…' He stopped and finally met her eyes. 'I'm afraid you'll have to talk to the King. He's altered the arrangements.'

'Yes?' Annalisa's skin prickled as that prescience of trouble grew stronger. 'How did he alter them?'

'He's cancelled them.'

Annalisa heard the words echo through her, felt their impact like the slow motion force of a traffic collision.

Blindly she groped for support, clutching the back of a chair with shaking fingers.

Only yesterday Tahir had referred to their wedding. Why change his mind? Had he read her neediness and her emotions even though she hadn't voiced them? Had he understood how she felt and decided to weather the scandal rather than lumber himself with a woman so obviously in love with him?

Had he rejected her because he couldn't accept her love? Because he couldn't return it?

'Here. Please! Sit down.' The secretary grabbed her elbow and guided her into a nearby chair.

Obediently Annalisa sank, grateful for the support as her knees turned to water.

'Are you absolutely sure?' She fixed him with a look that begged him to be wrong.

Hurriedly he shook his head. 'No, I'm sorry. His Majesty cancelled the arrangements only a few hours ago. Perhaps if you talk to him…?'

What? He'd agree to marry her after all?

From the first Tahir hadn't wanted marriage. He'd felt obligated. And now…now, for all their physical intimacy, perhaps she'd got too close to that part of himself he held so private.

Her heart throbbed pure pain. No doubt he thought it easier to provide financial support for their child than entangle himself with a needy woman.

'Wait there. I'll get you some tea.' Her companion hurried away, leaving Annalisa to stare at the cluster of gilded French antique furniture in the room. It reminded her inevitably of the huge gulf between her and Tahir.

Had she fooled herself with dreams of a love-match? How had she let herself think for a moment it was possible?

She tried to tell herself it was for the best, ending things now rather than going through the emotional entanglement of a doomed marriage.

Yet she couldn't convince herself.

She was still gazing dry-eyed before her, when a door slammed and she heard footsteps on the inlaid floor of the outer office.

'…and your personal leadership during this disaster has made all the difference, sire. Without it the relief operation would not have been so effective.'

'You flatter me, Akmal. But thank you. I realise I'm not the man the elders expected to have on the throne.'

'Let me assure you, your actions these past couple of months have won their respect. As will your decision to cancel that imprudent marriage. It's gratifying you've taken the advice of your counsellors on this issue.'

Annalisa pressed her palm to her mouth.

'If I'd taken your advice, Akmal, I'd be crowned already and married to a foreign princess with blue blood and ice in her veins.' Tahir's voice was terse.

The sound of it made Annalisa twist in her seat. But they couldn't see her. She was hidden by a carved screen inlaid with mother of pearl. Her stomach fluttered in distress. She didn't want to be here, listening to their discussion. But she couldn't face him. Not yet.

'I wish you'd stop delaying your coronation, sire. It's what the country needs. Stability, proof that the monarchy is solid and here to stay.'

'You don't think marrying the mother of my child indicates a certain permanency?'

Annalisa winced at the heavy irony in his tone.

'Laudable as your intentions were, Majesty, we both know the child can be brought up out of the limelight. With sufficient money it will be well cared for and educated. And if you wish to continue a discreet relationship with the mother…'

Nausea engulfed her, and she didn't hear the rest of the sentence for the buzzing sound in her ears. She hunched over, arms wrapped around her waist, breathing slowly through her nose in an attempt to force down the bile in her throat.

'Besides…' The other man's voice began to fade, presumably as they entered the inner office. 'Such a marriage isn't possible. The King must either marry royalty or a woman of pure Qusani blood. It's written in the constitution. This woman's father was Danish. She's not suitable as your consort.'

Annalisa barely heard the thud of heavy doors closing. Her mind was filled with the brutal words she'd not been meant to hear.

Tahir's advisor proposed to pay her off with cash then set her up somewhere so she could be the King's…what? Mistress? Concubine? Even for Qusay the idea was medieval.

As for the requirement for pure Qusani blood! Right now *her* blood, pure or not, was boiling at the man's attitude. How could he take such an antiquated view of the world? Hadn't he heard of the twenty-first century?

She shot to her feet and paced the small salon.

To be discussed as if she were a problem, a *thing* to be moved or used or discarded as they saw fit! To be rejected because she wasn't royal, or because her father had been born in Copenhagen! She was as much a Qusani as Tahir and his precious Akmal. More so. Unlike Tahir, she'd lived here all her life—and, unlike his advisor, not in a gilded palace but with ordinary Qusanis.

How dared they belittle her like that?

Fury surged in her bloodstream, propelling her across the room and out of the door.

She'd wondered if Tahir could ever love her and now she had her answer. Now she knew exactly what to do.

It was time to go home.

CHAPTER FIFTEEN

TAHIR strode down the frescoed corridor, eager to reach his destination.

The day had been difficult. The cleaning-up work after the earthquake continued, and organising emergency housing and supplies for the dispossessed was a massive undertaking.

Then there was the matter of his marriage.

He'd reckoned without the obstinacy of the Council of Elders, who stuck blindly to the old ways. They wanted him married, all right, but to a woman of their choosing. It was only today he'd learned exactly how far they'd take their opposition.

Strange how they were willing to accept him, a prodigal returned, as their monarch, but quibbled over his choice of wife.

He set his jaw, remembering his recent interview with Akmal. The vizier was determined to force his hand and manoeuvre him into marrying a princess.

Tahir slipped a hand into his trouser pocket, grasping it on the weighty package there. His lips curved in a smile of anticipation.

With this gift he planned to get everything he wanted from Annalisa.

'What's the meaning of this?' Tahir strode past the suitcase lying open on the bed, half full of her clothes. He followed the sound of movement into the nearby dressing room and slammed to a stop.

Annalisa stood there, wearing nothing but lace panties and bra. On the floor at her feet lay of pool of crimson silk embroidered with pearls. He recognised it instantly: a dress he'd ordered for Annalisa to go with the pearl and ruby diadem he'd present her with when they married. He'd asked his mother to give her the dress, knowing his fiancée, with her quaint scruples, would balk at accepting it from him.

Annalisa's face was chalky, her expression mutinous as she stared back at him. No mistaking the anger sparking in her gaze, nor the hurt tightening her mouth.

What had happened to the warm, accommodating woman he'd left in bed just hours ago?

'I'm leaving. That's what it means.'

She drew a deep breath, and despite his confusion he couldn't help appreciating the way her breasts lifted in their lace cups.

'And stop looking at me like that!' Her eyes flashed. 'I'm not a plaything for your enjoyment.' She stooped and retrieved the dress, holding it in front of her.

'You're not going anywhere.' The notion was unthinkable. He strode nearer and his blood ran cold as she backed away.

She shook her head and her unbound hair swirled around her bare shoulders, reminding him of the way she'd lain in his arms through the night. The way she'd made him feel: pleasured, triumphant, whole. Curiously at peace.

'I'm leaving and you can't stop me.' Her chin lifted in the sign of quiet resolution he knew so well.

'Annalisa?' A curious sensation began deep in his gut. A roiling, unsettled feeling he remembered from another time, another life.

Anxiety. *Fear*.

The notion of her walking out of his life made a yawning void open up before him. Worse than the agony he'd endured at his father's hands. Worse even than the blank grey nothingness that had haunted him before he came here.

Pain transfixed him, froze his heart as he read her bitterness and anger.

She couldn't go. He wouldn't allow it.

'Of course you'll stay.' He tried to sound reasonable, but the words emerged brusquely.

'No! What have I got to stay for?' She lifted her chin still higher in unconscious arrogance and Tahir's certainty crumbled.

'To be with me.'

Or had she decided he was too flawed? That he wasn't worth the risk? A man with a past like his had no right expecting a woman like Annalisa to want him. But he did. He had from the first.

She blinked, and he thought he saw her eyes glaze with tears. He started forward, but again she retreated.

'That's enough, you think?'

Her words pierced him to the core. He'd finally realised what he wanted from Annalisa, only to have her reject him out of hand.

He should accept her decision. An honourable man would. But Tahir had no pretensions to honour. Not if that meant letting her go.

His eyes blazed fire as he closed the gap between them, looming over her, all male aggression and power.

A tiny part of her revelled in the fact that he wanted her so badly, even though it was only for sex. As his mistress on the side. Even now she responded to him physically, wanted him so badly.

'Don't touch me!'

But it was too late. His hands curled round her shoulders, hauling her close so he engulfed her senses, his body hard against hers, the scent of his skin sabotaging her resolve.

'You love it when I touch you.' His look told her he knew her weakness and intended to make the most of it. He slid an arm around her bare back and secured her tightly.

The air around them shimmered with tension, with sparks of electricity, with combustible emotional energy.

'No!' She couldn't afford to give in now—not when she'd gathered the strength to do what she must.

But her resistance had no effect. He slipped his other hand over her breast, moulding it in a possessive grasp that sent desire shuddering through her.

How was she meant to withstand him when she couldn't fight her own weakness?

'Please, Tahir. No.' She squeezed her eyes shut and her head lolled as she arched instinctively in his hold, pressing wantonly for more.

'*Yes*, Annalisa. You *will* be mine. Whatever I have to do. Whatever it takes.' He dragged in a rough breath. 'I gave you up once before. At the oasis I deliberately baited and insulted you so you'd turn away and not look back. I didn't deserve you and I knew it, so for that day I became the sort of shallow bastard I knew you'd abhor.'

The urgency of his words, the deep hoarse timbre of his voice, mesmerised her.

'I owe you apologies for that. You don't know how it cut me to hurt you that day, when all I wanted was to drag you close and not release you.' Searing blue eyes met hers. '*But I can't do it again. I can't force myself to give you up. You can't expect it of me.*'

Was it true? Had his loutish behaviour been a ploy to scare her off? She could barely believe it. Yet it would explain the puzzling difference between his behaviour then and since. Could he have cared so much and behaved so foolishly?

Yet what did it change? Nothing.

She shook her head in mute desperation, knowing she had to escape before she succumbed to him again. But her body already betrayed her. With Tahir she lost the will for self-preservation. He even undermined her pride.

'I can't—'

'You can, Annalisa. You will.' He mouthed the words against her neck as he swept kisses over her throat.

'For how long, Tahir?' Anguish drew the words from her. 'How long will you want me as your mistress? How long before the next woman takes your fancy?'

He froze, hands tightening on her. She felt the heavy thud

of his heart through the thin fabric. Finally he raised his head and she met his curiously blank stare.

'There will be no other woman.' The words sounded like a vow. 'I've never wanted a woman the way I want you. I never *will* want another woman.

How self-delusional could she get? She shook her head, trying to dislodge the illusion that he meant it.

'So you say.' She spat the words out. 'Will you expect to keep me somewhere conveniently close and still come home to your royal wife?'

His head reared back as if struck. Dull colour mounted his high cheeks.

'What are you talking about? *You'll* be my wife.'

If she didn't know better she'd believe the confusion on his face. Even now it was a struggle to accept the truth. Tahir had never lied to her before.

'Don't.' She pushed fruitlessly against his broad chest. 'Don't pretend. I know you've cancelled the wedding. And I know why.' She turned her head, unable to meet his piercing gaze any longer. 'I know you can't marry me. I'm not *suitable*.' The word tasted bitter on her tongue.

All her life she'd been an outsider. Never more so than now, when she wasn't deemed good enough to marry the man she loved.

Tahir swore, long and low and comprehensively.

'Who told you that?' His voice sliced the air like a cold steel blade, raising the hairs on the back of her neck. 'Give me his name, Annalisa.'

She turned her head, shivering at the deadly intent she read in his taut features.

'Who was it?' His voice burred with barely veiled threat.

'I heard it with my own ears, Tahir. You and Akmal. There's no use pretending.'

He tugged her hard against him, arms encompassing her. 'I wouldn't have had you overhear that for anything.'

'No. I'm sure.' She tried to stand rigid within his embrace but it was impossible.

'I thought you'd decided you couldn't trust yourself and the baby to a man like me.' The echo of pain in his voice drew her skin tighter. 'That you hold my past against me.'

'No!' She was aghast he'd even think it. 'This isn't about trusting you as a father.'

Her throat closed as she realised how much she wanted him as a hands-on dad for their child.

'This isn't about you, Tahir. It's about me. About the fact that I won't make a suitable queen.' She lifted her head. 'And about the fact you don't want to marry me. Now, please,' she said, summoning the last of her pride, 'don't make this harder. Let me go.' Her voice wobbled and she bit her lip hard, striving for control.

Tahir stepped back and instantly she craved his touch. She wanted to burrow herself in his embrace and say she'd take whatever he'd give her, no matter how fleeting.

He stood proud and tall. A strong man. The man who owned her heart and soul. *The man who could never be hers.*

A sob rose in her chest and jammed her throat. She wrapped her arms round herself, hugging the crimson silk close, knowing her dream was over.

'You fill my life, Annalisa. You make me whole. *That's* what matters.'

Slowly, without taking his eyes from hers, Tahir reached into a pocket and drew out a velvet pouch embroidered with gold. He opened it, plunged his hand inside and withdrew something that shimmered fire.

'You will be the finest queen Qusay has known. Not just because of your compassion and intelligence. But because I love you, Annalisa.' He held out his hand. 'Do you hear me? I love you and I want you to be my wife. Not only for the sake of our child, but because I can't imagine my life without you by my side.'

He unfurled his fingers and a thousand scintillating lights dazzled her. Emeralds and diamonds spilled from his hand in a massive sparkling web.

Her breath stopped as she realised what it was: the Queen's Necklace. A royal symbol of power and wealth dating back centuries to the time, it was said, of the first emerald mines in Qusay. It was given to each new queen as a sign of her paramount place in the kingdom and of her husband's fidelity.

Annalisa's knees crumpled, and only Tahir's strong hands stopped her collapsing. Against one bare shoulder she felt the cold touch of peerless gems. They were real.

'Annalisa! Say something.' His voice was hoarse with passion.

'But you can't—' She struggled for words as she grappled to understand. 'You don't—'

'Love you? Of course I do.' His hands tightened against her. 'Can you forgive me for not realising sooner? It's still a new concept to me. But if knowing I never want to be anywhere but by your side means love, and wanting to grow old with you, watching our children and their children, then I love you.' He dragged in a huge breath. 'You make me dare to want what I never dreamed of before: the love of one special woman.'

Her heart swelled at the look in his eyes.

'The question is, do you trust me enough to be my wife?' A shadow of doubt darkened his clear blue gaze. 'I'll do my best to be a good husband. And I'll learn to be the sort of father our child needs.'

Annalisa had never seen him so earnest. Never before felt the emotion that flowed from him in warm waves. Love, strong and pure.

'Of course I trust you, Tahir.' She raised her hands and cupped his strong jaw. 'I love you. I've always loved you.' Fire blazed in his eyes and, emboldened, she leaned close to kiss him, her heart overflowing with a happiness she'd never thought possible.

'Wait! Let me do this first.'

Bewildered, she saw him lift one hand and turn her round. In the full-length mirror on the wall she saw their reflection. Tahir behind her, raising the net of stones, massive emeralds interspersed with teardrop diamonds, over her head.

The crimson dress had already dropped unheeded to the floor and she stood, naked but for her lace underwear, as he fastened the elegant necklace, a king's ransom, around her throat.

Her eyes widened at the weight of it, the sheer magnificence. But it was Tahir's hands, slipping round to undo her bra and tug it away, that absorbed her attention. The sight of them together, of his bronzed hands moving purposefully on her paler flesh, sent ripples of desire through her.

'My perfect bride,' he murmured against her neck as he cupped her breasts with warm hands.

Fire sizzled through her and she sagged back against him, eyes fluttering shut.

'But I'm not. I'm not royal. I'm half-foreign.'

'You're perfect,' he said again, nipping the sensitive flesh beneath her ear.

This time, hearing the love in his words, she dared to believe.

'That's why I cancelled the wedding arrangements. I realised last night I couldn't take you as my wife in some second-rate ceremony. I want the world to know when I make you my bride.' His breath was warm on her skin. 'It will take longer to arrange, but we're having the biggest wedding Qusay has ever seen.'

'But you can't. The constitution…' Her words petered out under the sheer weight of sensual pleasure as he massaged her breasts and kissed her bare shoulders.

'The constitution will be changed. If Qusay wants me as King, then you will be my Queen. I met with Akmal today to make my ultimatum, and believe me…' he paused on a chuckle '…I made my point forcefully. Arrangements are being made as we speak.' He nuzzled her neck. 'Now, open your eyes, *habibti.*'

Annalisa lifted heavy lids, attuned now to the telltale heat of his body behind hers and his rigid arousal pressing against her. She saw their reflection. The knowing gleam in her lover's bright gaze: his hands roving her body, almost bare but for the stunning, regal jewels. Then his hand dipped low.

'I want you to watch,' he whispered, 'as I make love to my fiancée.'

The wedding celebrations had taken seven days.

As Tahir had promised, they'd been the most lavish Qusay

had seen. Partly because he'd ensured all Qusanis were welcome to attend the entertainments, and partly because it had been a joint celebration.

On the fifth day his coronation had taken place.

Now he stood, a sea breeze rippling the magnificent embroidered cloak that hung from his shoulders, the unfamiliar weight of the royal black and gold *igal* encircling the fine white cloth of his headdress. At his side the King's Sword lay heavy against his thigh. An ancient symbol of the wealth and power of Qusay's ruler, its scabbard was encrusted with gems. Its hilt, weighted with emeralds the size of pigeon's eggs, belied the fact that the blade was sharp enough to wreak justice on any who threatened the King or his country.

He felt the weight of expectation and responsibility on him, but he carried it easily, confident now that he'd done the right thing in accepting the kingship.

Music swelled on the late-afternoon air and the hum of voices. The perfume of fragrant spices from elaborate braziers mixed with the scent of yet more roast meats being prepared.

Tahir drew a deep breath and surveyed the gathering. Throngs of people laughing and chattering, some beneath open-sided tents lined with carpets and padded seating. Others strolling in the gardens or watching the horse-racing down on the white sand beach. Pennants fluttered, jewels flashed, silks swirled.

Yet among the throng one person caught and held his attention. His heart swelled with that unfamiliar emotion he realised now was love.

Annalisa. His bride. His queen. His love.

Her smile had been radiant all day, first with her cousins, who'd been genuinely happy for her, and now with his family.

'You've got that look on your face again, Tahir,' came a deep voice beside him. 'Didn't you know a king is supposed to look solemn and regal?'

Tahir's lips twitched and he turned to his brother Rafiq, looking debonair in a dark suit. 'Much you'd know about it. You were never King.'

Rafiq shrugged. 'What can I say? I had a better offer.' His eyes strayed to the cluster of beautiful women just metres away.

'You were saying? About that look?' Tahir laughed. It was a sound he'd become gradually used to these past few months, as his world had filled with a warmth and happiness he'd never take for granted.

'Oh, don't pay any attention to him,' said Kareef as he strolled up to join them, a glint of humour in his pale blue eyes. 'You know he's got it bad. Can't keep his eyes off his wife.'

'Which makes four of us, and you wouldn't want it any other way.' Their cousin Zafir came to stand on Tahir's other side. He raised a hand and the sun glinted off his sapphire ring. He gestured towards the cluster of women in the royal tent. 'We've been lucky, all of us.'

There was a murmur of assent from deep voices.

Tahir scanned the group. Zafir's Layla, dripping sapphires and dressed in regal finery, yet with a smile as warm as the sun. Rafiq's Serah, with her quiet beauty and gentle nature, now laughing with her childhood friend Jasmine, Kareef's lovely wife.

And his mother was there, looking happier than he'd ever seen her, matriarch of a growing family. For at their centre sat the most beautiful of them all: his Annalisa, cradling Jasmine and Kareef's tiny adopted daughter.

At the sight of his wife holding the infant so tenderly heat roared through him, a proud possessiveness he felt whenever he thought of the child she carried. Beneath her exquisite dress of silver her once-flat belly had begun to swell with the weight of their child.

He longed to reach out and stroke that satiny flesh with his palm, reacquaint himself with each luscious curve and line of her body. They hadn't shared a bed in seven nights, mindful for once of tradition. But tonight…

As if reading his thoughts, Annalisa lifted her head and met his gaze head-on. A delicate blush stained her cheeks and her lips parted in unconscious invitation.

Tahir almost groaned aloud.

He wanted to stride over, slip the dress from her shoulders and make love to her as she wore nothing but the emerald and diamond collar. As he had the day he'd first put it on her. An image of Annalisa naked but for the gems filled his mind. Pliant and sexy under his questing hands, soft and welcoming against his hard flesh. A shudder of pure need racked him.

Saying something to the other women, Annalisa passed the baby over and rose, a shimmering vision in her wedding dress. Late sun caught the golden lights in her hair as she walked towards him. Her gown sparkled with embroidered gems. Her jewelled chandelier earrings swayed against her pale neck, accentuating its slender curve.

Slowly she approached. Their gazes meshed.

He heard voices beside him and realised his companions were moving away, leaving him alone with his bride. His family showed the good sense to know when a man needed to be alone with his wife.

Then she was before him. Velvet eyes gazed up with a stunned delight he knew matched his own expression.

'You look like an impatient bridegroom,' she said, her voice husky.

'I am.' He claimed her, wrapping his hand around hers and drawing her close. 'I want you so badly it hurts to breathe.'

Her lips curved in an enchanting smile, even as her eyes gleamed with excitement. 'Then perhaps we should leave everyone to their celebrations, so I can…tend your hurts.'

Tahir sucked in a deep breath at the image her words conjured.

'Soon,' he promised, 'when I'm capable of walking.' He pulled her to him and turned her round so she stood, like him, looking out over the colourful scene. She fitted against his body, into his arms, as if made for him.

'No regrets about becoming my Queen?'

'Of course not.' She shook her head and the delicate scent of cinnamon and wild honey teased his nostrils.

Beneath the finery she was still the woman he'd met in the desert. Capable, loving, wonderful. His arms closed round her tenderly.

'I love you,' he whispered against her hair.

'And I love you, Tahir. Always.' She wrapped her hands over his encompassing arms and sank against him.

He and Annalisa would be together for the rest of their lives. He'd never known such happiness.

HARLEQUIN *Presents*

Coming Next Month

in **Harlequin Presents® EXTRA.** Available July 13, 2010.

#109 HIRED FOR THE BOSS'S BEDROOM
Cathy Williams
Her Irresistible Boss

#110 THE COUNT OF CASTELFINO
Christina Hollis
Her Irresistible Boss

#111 RULING SHEIKH, UNRULY MISTRESS
Susan Stephens
P.S. I'm Pregnant!

#112 MISTRESS: AT WHAT PRICE?
Anne Oliver
P.S. I'm Pregnant!

Coming Next Month

in **Harlequin Presents®.** Available July 27, 2010.

#2933 THE ITALIAN DUKE'S VIRGIN MISTRESS
Penny Jordan

#2934 MIA AND THE POWERFUL GREEK
Michelle Reid
The Balfour Brides

#2935 THE GREEK'S PREGNANT LOVER
Lucy Monroe
Traditional Greek Husbands

#2936 AN HEIR FOR THE MILLIONAIRE
Julia James and Carole Mortimer
2 in 1

#2937 COUNT TOUSSAINT'S BABY
Kate Hewitt

#2938 MASTER OF THE DESERT
Susan Stephens

LARGER-PRINT BOOKS!

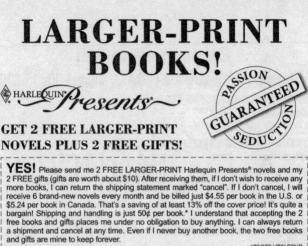

HARLEQUIN *Presents*~

PASSION
GUARANTEED
SEDUCTION

GET 2 FREE LARGER-PRINT NOVELS PLUS 2 FREE GIFTS!

YES! Please send me 2 FREE LARGER-PRINT Harlequin Presents® novels and my 2 FREE gifts (gifts are worth about $10). After receiving them, if I don't wish to receive any more books, I can return the shipping statement marked "cancel". If I don't cancel, I will receive 6 brand-new novels every month and be billed just $4.55 per book in the U.S. or $5.24 per book in Canada. That's a saving of at least 13% off the cover price! It's quite a bargain! Shipping and handling is just 50¢ per book.* I understand that accepting the 2 free books and gifts places me under no obligation to buy anything. I can always return a shipment and cancel at any time. Even if I never buy another book, the two free books and gifts are mine to keep forever.

176/376 HDN E5NG

Name _____ (PLEASE PRINT) _____

Address _____ Apt. # _____

City _____ State/Prov. _____ Zip/Postal Code _____

Signature (if under 18, a parent or guardian must sign)

Mail to the **Harlequin Reader Service:**
IN U.S.A.: P.O. Box 1867, Buffalo, NY 14240-1867
IN CANADA: P.O. Box 609, Fort Erie, Ontario L2A 5X3

Not valid for current subscribers to Harlequin Presents Larger-Print books.

**Are you a subscriber to Harlequin Presents books
and want to receive the larger-print edition?
Call 1-800-873-8635 today!**

* Terms and prices subject to change without notice. Prices do not include applicable taxes. Sales tax applicable in N.Y. Canadian residents will be charged applicable provincial taxes and GST. Offer not valid in Quebec. This offer is limited to one order per household. All orders subject to approval. Credit or debit balances in a customer's account(s) may be offset by any other outstanding balance owed by or to the customer. Please allow 4 to 6 weeks for delivery. Offer available while quantities last.

Your Privacy: Harlequin Books is committed to protecting your privacy. Our Privacy Policy is available online at www.eHarlequin.com or upon request from the Reader Service. From time to time we make our lists of customers available to reputable third parties who may have a product or service of interest to you. If you would prefer we not share your name and address, please check here. ☐

Help us get it right—We strive for accurate, respectful and relevant communications. To clarify or modify your communication preferences, visit us at www.ReaderService.com/consumerschoice.

HPLP10R

HARLEQUIN®

A Romance

FOR EVERY MOOD™

Spotlight on

Heart & Home

Heartwarming romances
where love can happen
right when you least expect it.

See the next page to enjoy a sneak peek
from Harlequin® American Romance®,
a Heart and Home series.

Five hunky Texas single fathers—five stories from
Cathy Gillen Thacker's LONE STAR DADS *miniseries.*
Here's an excerpt from the latest, THE MOMMY PROPOSAL
from Harlequin American Romance.

"I hear you work miracles," Nate Hutchinson drawled.
Brooke Mitchell had just stepped into his lavishly appointed
office in downtown Fort Worth, Texas.

"Sometimes, I do." Brooke smiled and took the sexy
financier's hand in hers, shook it briefly.

"Good." Nate looked her straight in the eye. "Because
I'm in need of a home makeover—fast. The son of an old
friend is coming to live with me."

She was still tingling from the feel of his warm palm.
"Temporarily or permanently?"

"If all goes according to plan, I'll adopt Landry by
summer's end."

Brooke had heard the founder of Nate Hutchinson
Financial Services was eligible, wealthy and generous to a
fault. She hadn't known he was in the market for a family,
but she supposed she shouldn't be surprised. But Brooke
had figured a man as successful and handsome as Nate
would want one the old-fashioned way. *Not that this was
any of her business…*

"So what's the child like?" she asked crisply, trying not
to think how the marine-blue of Nate's dress shirt deepened
the hue of his eyes.

"I don't know." Nate took a seat behind his massive
antique mahogany desk. He relaxed against the smooth
leather of the chair. "I've never met him."

"Yet you've invited this kid to live with you permanently?"

"It's complicated. But I'm sure it's going to be fine."

Obviously Nate Hutchinson knew as little about teenage

boys as he did about decorating. But that wasn't her problem. Finding a way to do the assignment without getting the least bit emotionally involved was.

Find out how a young boy brings Nate and Brooke together in THE MOMMY PROPOSAL, coming August 2010 from Harlequin American Romance.

THE HEAT IS ON

by

Jill Shalvis

The attraction between Bella and
Detective Madden is undeniable.
But can a few wild encounters
turn into love?

Don't miss this hot read.

*Available in August
where books are sold.*

---

red-hot reads

www.eHarlequin.com

HB79562

The Balfour Brides

*A powerful dynasty,
eight daughters in disgrace…*

Absolute scandal has rocked the core of the infamous
Balfour family. The glittering, gorgeous daughters are in
disgrace…. Banished from the Balfour mansion, they're
sent to the boldest, most magnificent men
to be wedded, bedded…and tamed!

And so begins a scandalous saga of dazzling glamour
and passionate surrender.

Beginning August 2010

MIA AND THE POWERFUL GREEK—*Michelle Reid*
KAT AND THE DAREDEVIL SPANIARD—*Sharon Kendrick*
EMILY AND THE NOTORIOUS PRINCE—*India Grey*
SOPHIE AND THE SCORCHING SICILIAN—*Kim Lawrence*
ZOE AND THE TORMENTED TYCOON—*Kate Hewitt*
ANNIE AND THE RED-HOT ITALIAN—*Carol Mortimer*
BELLA AND THE MERCILESS SHEIKH—*Sarah Morgan*
OLIVIA AND THE BILLIONAIRE CATTLE KING—*Margaret Way*

8 volumes to collect and treasure!